KOMODO

JOHN LEE SCHNEIDER

SEVERED PRESS

HOBART TASMANIA

KOMODO

"So tomorrow we disappear into the unknown."

The Lost World
Sir Arthur Conan Doyle

CHAPTER 1

The wave came out of nowhere.

Marcus was alone on deck and the only one who saw it coming. Not that there was anything he could particularly *do* about it.

Rogue waves were once believed to be myth, but were now recognized by science to be fairly common, occurring many times a day in every ocean. They were known for striking with a freakish force that swamped and rolled full-sized cargo ships.

This one was coming right at them.

At its highest point, the fifty-foot yacht rose above the waterline over twenty-feet. Marcus estimated the rushing wall of water as easily twice that.

He had, of course, *heard* of rogue waves – just as he had heard about great white sharks, and saltwater crocodiles – but he had never expected to see one of *those* up close either. He'd gotten a good look at both on this trip – among other things – and they had all scared the hell out of him.

Now, as he stood there, a hapless land-dwelling hominid, who had somehow managed to find himself dead in the middle of an empty ocean, a hemisphere from home, watching the sea rear itself up like a thing alive, counting down what might be his last few ticking seconds on Earth, his life *did* pass before his eyes – and he tried to remember why *any* of this had seemed like a good idea.

Irony on irony, he had just finished thinking he *must* have bottomed out – because his last-ditch, save-the-marriage world-tour was already in tatters.

That was, in fact, why he'd come up on deck – to try and convince himself it wasn't over.

But his wife Anna had been telling him so for over a year, in every way except verbally. This ill-advised jaunt around the world only made it more vivid.

Marcus had been hoping the doldrums between islands might provide a little alone time, some forced proximity. Instead, Anna had taken ill – seasick or stomach flu – and she'd been up vomiting all night.

Frustratingly, she just wanted to be left alone. That was what she always wanted from him these days.

Now, it was early in the morning, and as far as Marcus knew, everybody else was still asleep. Anna's BFF, Mona – 'Watson' now, on her third last name, following 'Mills' and the original 'Jacobson' – had invited herself and her latest post-divorce boy-toy along for the trip. They had both been drinking the night before and had not yet stirred.

Mona was actually the catalyst that set-up this whole trip – all those afternoon wine-and-bitch sessions, with an open bottle, soap-operas in the background, and all the greatest hits of yesteryear playing on the stereo.

She told Anna, "You need an adventure."

Marcus had learned to be wary whenever Mona initiated one of these little kernels in casual conversation – any flight of fancy might flare randomly out of control, into quick and intense obsessions that burned as hot as they were fickle – cue her own marriages.

Her latest sponsor (Marcus' private word) was called 'Rodger Vaughn'. Like all Mona's paramours, he was well-to-do – he mentioned a tech-repair company. He was the sort who introduced himself by his full name with a pump-handshake. No doubt simply having fun with his latest hottie, in-between his own divorces, the poor guy had no idea how close he was to the wood-chipper.

The last man on board was, of course, Captain Colin, who owned the boat.

Rugged. Handsome. Now, *this* guy, Anna had been paying attention to.

Marcus wondered how much Mona had to do with setting *that* up as well.

As Anna's friend, and pointedly not Marcus', why *wouldn't* she? After all, she had to sense the same thing Marcus did.

It was the most frustrating, depressing thing, yet implacable, simple reality – his wife just didn't love him anymore.

The hell of it was, she still dazzled him. As much as the moment he had met her – senior year at UCLA, in a college bar – the smart best-friend of the aggressive floozy.

Anna was one of those girls who just looked sexy as hell in glasses – like a hot, nerdy-librarian in a *Playboy* spread. And she actually worked at the campus library, pulling straight A's in academic subjects like folklore and classical literature – a sheltered bookworm with a head-full of mythical romance and adventure.

Ten years later, she still carried the look of a college girl – relaxed and comfortable in a barely-there bikini, and the slight extra plumpness of maturity only added a saucy accent to her curves.

That was another backfire of the cruise portion of their trip – it made it all the more painfully obvious Marcus had married up. After all these years, that bothersome little fact finally seemed to be dawning on Anna herself.

And if this dawning seemed to coincide with Marcus' lost job – his whole industry, such as it was – and with it, any immediate financial bounce-back...?

Well, perhaps that abiding fact *should* make him angry.

Not that Anna would overtly complain – she didn't have tantrums, she didn't pester or belittle. She just decided to be really unhappy ALL the time.

Marcus' father once told him that the male/female relationship was very simple – each of them had a job to do – *he* had to make her happy, and *she* had to make him *want* to. If either of those things weren't happening, the relationship would deteriorate.

Well, *he* still wanted to. That meant she was doing her job. He just had to figure out how to do his.

Nothing he'd tried had worked so far, and this expensive world-adventure seemed to be driving things to a head.

Instead of her normal, introvert self, Anna was indulging the opportunity to act out, and it manifested in a recklessness as unpredictable as it was out of character.

For a woman who looked disapprovingly after speeders, and frowned on violent sports, she'd gone utterly half-cocked. Croc-parks, river-tours – for God's sake, *cage diving*?

Marcus had, admittedly, promised adventure. *Him* – north California suburbia – an economics major. Indiana Jones, he was not.

He had more in mind like eating foreign food in an actual foreign restaurant.

At this point, Marcus desperately did not want any more adventures. Like any good story, they were always much better when they happened to someone else.

The 'croc-river' tour alone – he had thought *that* was bad – the way those big, deceptively lazy reptiles suddenly reared up six and eight feet – easily your own shoulder height, sitting in the boat, separated by a ridiculously thin rail bar – even as the tour guide casually dangled bite-sized chickens out on a line.

That was *before* the cage diving.

Marcus had let Anna drag him to a number of scuba-classes last summer – just as he had accompanied her to work-out sessions, dance lessons, painful and humiliating karate classes – having *no clue* what he was setting himself up for. While he would have been agreeable to just about anything he thought would please her, it was an entirely different perspective once he found himself trapped in a cage, with fourteen and fifteen-foot great white sharks mouthing at the bars.

Gosh, he remembered thinking, as the teeth gnawed the cage, this is the *stupidest* thing I've ever done.

He wouldn't let himself back out.

And *no*, he would tell anyone who asked, for the rest of his life, it was *not* fun at *all*.

3

He had drained his air-tank too quickly and stayed down until he began getting light-headed, just to show how terrified he wasn't. It was all he could do not to collapse to the floorboards of the boat, once they were finally brought back up.

Anna seemed to love every minute of it. Unfortunately, it seemed to be in all the wrong ways.

Rather than sharing an adventure, it was more like an escape... from *him*.

For the first time, Marcus was considering giving up.

Wasn't that the kind thing? If you loved someone, let them go?

Marcus was pretty sure, once he let her go, Anna wouldn't be coming back.

Which, he supposed, was the point. She had lost faith in him as a man.

And just to add another acidic dose of irony, it occurred to him that her behavior all along this trip was not really recklessness at all, so much as blind trust – the sort a passenger extends to a pilot – or a ride in a theme park.

Or more accurately, the trust Jane has in Tarzan.

Marcus was nobody's Tarzan, but he recognized clearly who was. And it was as if he'd gone out of his way to provide one, made-to-order, for his pretty, unhappy wife.

Colin. 'Captain' Colin these days. Colin 'Braddock' no less – their guide since they'd touched down in the Australian mainland.

They had all been friends in college – yesterday and forever ago.

When Anna had fallen seasick, Captain Colin had been dutifully concerned. Out on the ocean, with no immediate aid available, even mild ailments could become serious, and he had been tending to her professionally.

Which, of course, left Marcus' job to stay out of the way.

Anna would trust Colin in a way she would never trust him.

Although to be fair, Marcus had known Colin a long time, and felt the same way. It was more or less presumption that, whatever the situation, Colin could handle it.

His boat's name said it all – 'The Challenger'.

The name actually sparked an amusing exchange when they'd first boarded, after Mona – blatantly flirtatious, Rodger or no Rodger – had asked, "Why would you name a boat after a shuttle that exploded?"

Colin had raised an arched brow. "Actually, it's Professor Challenger, from 'The Lost World'."

He turned and waved out at the open ocean.

"You see, these waters are the most prehistoric part of the planet. Islands out here have still got dinosaurs on them. Or just as good. A big ol' crocodile bites like a baby *T. rex*."

Colin nodded out over Darwin Harbor.

"There are crocs are out there right now. Trust me, you never want to tarry around the water's edge in Northern Australia."

Mona looked uncomfortably down at the muddy brown surface.

Colin smiled. "And that's just here on the mainland. Out around the islands, they've got critters running around that have lived in isolation for a million years. It's the land that *forgot* about the Land That Time Forgot."

Colin tapped the painted stencils on his ship's bow.

"I guess when you're going out into a world like that, you pick a name that helps you feel brave. When small things like that might make the difference."

But then he stroked his chin, considering.

"Although," he said, "I never really made the space-shuttle connection before. Now that I think about it, that *is* kind of bad association."

He turned and looked at Mona seriously.

"I hope you haven't put the hex on us. We don't play around with omens out on the sea."

Mona stared back, wide-eyed.

Colin held his grim face a moment longer before breaking back into his easy grin.

"*But*...., we'll probably be fine." He slapped the hull. "All aboard, folks."

Marcus had snickered. The guy was hard not to like.

Colin was a few years older than the rest of them. He had been at UCLA for his grad studies – oceanography, or some-such – specifically related to Navy SEAL-type stuff – or the Australian Special Forces counterpart. Colin and Marcus belonged to the same fraternity, and Marcus had held him in the same reverent awe as everyone else.

He was definitely good to have around – especially with Marcus being the sort that, for whatever reason, people felt comfortable beating-up on – a condition that got worse with alcohol. One particular night, he'd found himself backed up against a wall outside their apartment by some rough-housing footballers, drunk on a Saturday night.

Things escalated quickly. Marcus himself had been just drunk enough to talk back, which activated the alcohol-stimulated response.

Colin had ambled up on the scene and tapped mildly on the wall – not even saying anything – he just made a 'scat' sound with his teeth.

The leader, a big beefy linebacker, who Marcus had seen in the papers, took umbrage, and stepped forward to engage. Colin knocked him out *cold* – one punch, with the sort of casual movement Marcus would have used to swat at an annoying fly.

Colin had shrugged, smiling good-naturedly, as the linebacker's friends stared back wide-eyed.

"Seriously, fellas," he said, "I ain't even mad, yet."

Without further comment, they gathered up their fallen friend, and retreated to safer parts of campus.

Colin was also good to be around once the females started circling – he attracted a lot of them, but there was only one of him.

In point of fact, that was how Marcus had met Anna.

It was also not the least reason he and Colin hadn't kept in more than rudimentary contact in the years since.

Marcus was aware Anna was impressed with Colin. That wasn't unusual, or even that worrisome – ALL the girls liked Colin. Marcus' own mother had once commented, "Your friend Colin is *very* good-looking."

The thing Marcus knew about Anna, however, was that she preferred 'safe danger' – she was the girl that fawned over the war-veteran *after* he got home from combat.

Colin was Tarzan for a living, and that was *way* too much first-hand for Anna's taste. So Marcus hadn't worried, not even when they seemed to hit it off during that forced-awkward, friend-of-the-boyfriend, six-or-seven months before Colin had gone back home.

But in the time since, Anna had talked about him a lot. Colin might have been too much adventure to live with, but he was perfect for a pining fantasy life.

This was the period where Marcus let his correspondence with his old college friend quietly fade. Because, while Marcus' own prospects had appeared good at the time – the safe economics-major with a solid future – once the mundane doldrums of everyday marriage set in... well, there was no sense inviting temptation.

Of course, without that specific fixation, that left a roving eye.

As was Anna's way, it was never overt. He would turn to see her glance back at him instead of the muscular fellow in gym-gear standing in the next aisle in the grocery store. Or the handsome waiter in the restaurant.

Marcus was not ugly, but he was not *handsome* – he was *cute*.

Like a puppy, he was cute.

But he was nobody's Tarzan.

Once, he had been able to compensate. After the basic mating instinct, there was also that all-important nesting instinct. That's where Marcus had his bases covered.

Except now? Not so much.

The thing was, while he got good grades, he was no entrepreneur. He was basically a bean-counter, and when the banking industry stumbled, and suddenly there were a handful of firms instead of dozens, that was when Marcus realized he didn't know how to *do* anything.

Any kid out of college could do finances, and while he might be able to work his way up the chain somewhere, counting beans with his calculator, it was a far cry away from the junior executive lifestyle he'd saddled himself with – the one his pretty wife had come to expect.

So what does he do?

He decides to spend tens of thousands on a worldwide cruise to show his unhappy wife the things he could no longer afford, putting himself in debt, and practically parading alpha males in front of her, all along the way.

As he stood there on deck that morning, he had been trying to remember back when he felt *smart*.

In a way, it was ironic that Marcus was the one that saw the wave when it hit. He never saw *anything* coming.

But on those odd occasions when he did, it did him little good. It was more like watching a punch coming in slow-motion, unable to move.

This was like *that*.

One moment, he had been standing there, alone on deck, feeling sorry for himself, moping on his own pathetic little world, with the entirety of the ocean around him, the most powerful ecological force on Earth, no more than scenery. Then, in the space of seconds, that same ocean suddenly and without warning, rose up to announce itself as a full and active participant in his personal reality.

Marcus' first reactive thought was that it looked like the feeding shows back at the croc-park – the way the calm, apparently empty surface suddenly erupted as the giant reptile launched half its length clear of the water, lunging with snapping, jagged teeth.

Or in this case, like some giant sea monster, reaching up with watery claws.

Marcus had been raised in a world where emergencies were solved by pulling alarms, making phone calls, or pushing buttons.

In the moments available, there were no buttons handy.

All that was left was simply to cry out – his voice shrill, hoarse. No words escaped – just a loud guttural shriek, his voice lost in the roar of the ocean.

He might have been trying to shout out, "*Hang on!*"

The wave hit.

CHAPTER 2

Marcus had time to think about the white sharks and the way they had mouthed the cage – and how puny they now seemed, like little guppies, next to the primal force that, for whatever reason, God or fate had sent their way.

Rogue waves could strike with a force of a hundred tons per square meter – it was not like getting hit by water. Marcus might have actually fared better if he'd been below decks. As it was, he was knocked nearly unconscious.

The boat rolled. Marcus had a bleary sense of light and dark, as he was rolled underwater with it.

He was taken deep – which probably saved his life, because he only held his breath through unconscious reflex, and if he'd been tossed with the wave, he would have surely inhaled water and drowned.

As it was, he popped to the surface, hanging limp and semi-conscious – a 'dead-man's float' – one of the first things he'd learned in swimming lessons back in Kindergarten.

Reflexively, he blew bubbles, and then started awake, sputtering, his head still ringing from heavy impact.

Over the ringing, he heard screams – Mona's voice.

After that was Colin. "Everybody! Sound off! Shout out wherever you are!"

Over the waves, Marcus heard Rodger. "Jesus! What the hell happened?"

Still dazed, Marcus found his own voice, reedy and weak. "Over here!"

As the ocean crested, he saw Colin had collared Mona, and seemed to have found one of those donut life-preservers. Rodger was paddling towards them.

The swells were large, but the sea had calmed.

"Freak wave," Colin shouted out, waving to Marcus, who struggled towards them.

Colin looked around. "Where's Anna?"

Marcus blanched. "Oh my God... she was down below..."

Without a word, Colin jack-knifed underwater.

The boat had been completely submerged, dragged down twenty-feet and drifting deeper.

Colin churned bubbles in his wake as he kicked after it.

Knowing it was already impossible, Marcus took a breath and followed.

The deepest water he'd ever swam in was the city pool, and once he dropped below ten feet, he felt the pressure like a weight, pushing at his eyes and ears, threatening to burst a lung.

He thought of his wife – trapped in the dark – drowning.

The boat was an indistinct mass.

His ears pounding, Marcus kicked until he felt the upturned hull touch his hand.

But he wasn't going to make it. Thirty more seconds and he would suck water and drown. He stared down helplessly.

Then Marcus saw movement, and Colin appeared from beneath the sinking hull, Anna crooked under one arm.

Without waiting, Marcus turned to struggle for the surface.

Colin passed him, and he could see Anna kicking of her own accord, alive and conscious.

His oxygen fading quickly, Marcus thrashed the last few desperate feet with all four limbs. His head broke the surface and he gasped for air.

The first thing he heard was Anna sobbing. "Oh my God. Oh my God."

Then Colin's voice. "Caught in an air-pocket. You were so lucky."

And Mona. "Oh *honey*, I thought you were gone."

The ocean swell finally crested high enough to spot the group of them, and Marcus called out.

Paddling up close, he reached out, nearly numb with relief, clasping his wife next to him in the water. "Oh thank *God*."

Anna accepted his embrace. But Marcus felt a little pull-back. Even now.

Then she turned to Colin.

"Thank you," she said. "For saving my life."

Rodger, however, was not convinced.

"Not to put a damper," he said, "but he might not have done that yet."

For a long moment, as the four of them clung to the single small donut, the only sound was the wind over the ocean.

"Seriously," Rodger said, looking around, "how screwed are we?"

They all turned to Colin, who gave it to them directly.

"Honestly?" he said. "Pretty screwed."

He covered his eyes in the sun, trying to get a look at the horizon.

"*But,*" he allowed, "not *totally*."

"What does that mean?" Mona asked.

"It means we can easily die right now. And if we want to live, we're going to have to do the work."

He pointed east. "The good news is, it's doable. This is a tight cluster of islands. Banta Island is only five miles out. That's our best chance, riding this current. There's a bay with dive-tours, and fishermen coming and going." He shrugged optimistically. "We might even get picked up on the way."

Marcus looked due east. All *he* could see was ocean. At water-level, the rising and falling swells hid anything that might lie beyond.

"Five miles," Colin said. "Ten minutes in a car. An hour on foot."

He crooked an eye at the others. "We've got a day ahead of us people."

A day, Marcus thought. Maybe into the night.

Five miles. Assuming they found the island at all.

Then there was that pesky ecology.

How had Colin described it? The biggest, meanest on the planet.

Within the hour, they saw the first shark.

CHAPTER 3

"That's a big one," Colin said.

Marcus blinked, images of his cage diving trauma blinking in strobe-light flashes of fresh memory.

When the wave hit, he had compared them to guppies. This was clearly punishment, because *now*, he was recalling how BIG their mouths were – the way they had mouthed the bars experimentally – not with any real intent, but Marcus could see very well what would happen if those teeth could reach just a few inches further.

Now he stared at the three-foot fin as it nonchalantly broke the surface, and he actually *felt* his body-temperature drop. He wondered how many more were down there, circling unseen, somewhere below their feet.

Colin had salvaged bits of flotsam from the wreck – a second preserver donut, which they lashed together, along with a boat-hook and a loose duffel that contained a pair of swim-fins and some eye goggles. He had promptly donned both, now kicking with a little more propulsion.

Over the last hour, he had been periodically pulling on the goggles and submerging, only to pop up a minute later.

Marcus couldn't see much below their feet, but noted Colin was staying close.

The first time, Rodger had asked, "What was that about?"

"Nothing to worry about," Colin replied evasively.

Then he had crowded them close on the two floating donuts.

"Stay together," he said.

He'd ducked below twice more after that. No one had questioned him again.

But now, as the fin circled their perimeter, he said quietly, "Don't panic. They've been scouting us for a while."

That, Marcus realized, was what Colin had been poking at down below – warding off the first inquisitive feelers, or else one of them might have already felt one of those investigatory 'tastes' on their dangling lower leg.

Marcus pulled closer to Anna, who suddenly sucked in breath, pointing.

A second fin had joined the first, circling further out.

Mona's voice was trilling out in a low, intelligible groan. Rodger hissed through his teeth, "Oh Jesus."

"Stay *calm*," Colin insisted. "And stay together. Great Whites are finicky. They won't waste energy on an attack unless they think they're going to get fair returns on the calories. Bony humans barely have the protein worth the metabolic effort to digest."

Then he hefted his boat hook. "Of course," he said, "you don't want them to figure that out *after* they've spat you out."

Colin kept his eyes steady on both fins at once.

"See?" he said. "They're just checking us out. They might try to sidle in for a nibble, but they're being careful. They don't charge seals in groups. That's a lot of canines coming back at you. They wait until they can isolate one of them by itself."

Now he was nodding confidently, holding his boat hook below the surface, aimed unerringly in the direction of the circling fins.

"If we stick together, they probably won't launch any of those Polaris attacks. Probably."

"But they *could*?" Mona persisted.

Colin sighed.

"Well, sure they could," he said. "But at this point, it's just easier to wait until we die of drowning or dehydration, and we're just floating meat to be eaten. Unless they're *really* hungry, that is."

Mona glanced unhappily at the surrounding water.

"Of course," Colin continued, "there are probably other sharks too. White-tips, tigers, bulls. They can all be pretty aggressive. Hell, we might even bump into the odd migrating crocodile.

"Or," he said, snapping his fingers, "there's snakes. Or *sea wasps* – those are jellyfish. If we run into a school of those, we're all dead in about sixty-seconds."

He leveled his glare at Mona impatiently.

"Feel better?"

Mona stared back, wide-eyed, shrinking against Rodger's side. Anna allowed Marcus to pull her close.

At the perimeter, one of the fins had dropped out of sight.

No doubt, it was circling below. Colin dipped his head beneath the surface, scanning the gloom with his goggles.

Visibility was already limited. What would happen after it got dark?

Anna was coughing. Marcus could feel her body convulse with spasms of nausea.

Could the sharks smell that she was sick? He knew they were attracted to vibrations, and she had been hacking and coughing.

When he looked up, Marcus realized the second circling fin had disappeared as well.

"Are they gone?" Mona whispered.

"I doubt it," Colin said. "Stay together."

Anna choked again, coughing up swallowed water. She'd already emptied any food from her stomach the night before.

There were dark circles under her eyes. Marcus cut a nervous glance at Colin, who nodded imperceptibly.

"Let's get moving folks. We've got to get there."

Marcus still could see nothing on the horizon.

For a long time, they simply fought the current.

So far, the circling fins had not reappeared.

But even more than the wolf, it was the shark you couldn't see...

And soon enough, it would be getting dark.

CHAPTER 4

Once night came, it lasted forever.

It was indescribable, out on the ocean, blinded in the sort of pitch blackness you simply never encountered in the suburbs.

Tonight there was cloud cover, not even any blinking stars.

Marcus knew that was bad. Colin had intended to navigate by the stars. Even the moon only showed itself in patches. They had no idea where the current was taking them.

Nobody spoke. Everybody's eyes and ears were tuned to the slightest odd splash.

To say nothing of that tickly feeling of displaced water, just beneath your feet.

Anna was fading. She continued to convulse in dry heaves, and by the time the sun had set, she was barely clinging to the preserver. Marcus locked his hand over her own. On her other side, Mona held a steady hand on her shoulder.

Colin kept his boat hook handy, his eyes watchful in the dark.

Marcus could have ticked every second – long hours of terrifying nothing, as they remained, as yet, unmolested.

But it was still the ocean itself that was the bigger threat. They *might* get bit by a shark, they *might* get stung by a jellyfish. But if they couldn't find land, they *would* become exhausted and drown.

Sooner than later – by the first light of morning, Marcus' hands latched over the preserver had gone numb. Anna's head lolled with drifting consciousness.

The early morning sun cast a reddish tint through the prism of gathered clouds.

Red sky at morning, Marcus thought dismally.

But the rising sun actually seemed to drive the clouds away. And once the sun had assumed its perch, Colin suddenly perked up, pointing east, squinting against the reflecting water.

"We've got land, people," he said. "About a mile out."

On the horizon, Marcus could now just barely see the crest of hills.

"That's gotta be Banta," Colin said. "We're going to make it."

Mona's breath let out in a reedy half-sob. "Oh thank *God*."

Marcus felt a new burst of energy, as hope rekindled itself. He tugged at Anna's shoulder, and was gratified as she attempted a smile.

On her other shoulder, Mona was in her ear. "Hang in there, girl. We're almost there."

"We're not out of the woods yet," Colin said. We've still got the currents. They can sweep us right by the island. It we get taken out past the cape, we'll be back in open ocean."

He pointed. "We have to come in from the north – ride the current – let it take us inland before we pass the south shore."

Colin's energy-conserving movements kicked up a notch.

"Now's the time to work, folks. Any calories you've got left, now's the time to burn them."

The ocean, however, had no intention of helping. The current was every bit as strong as they could have feared, and moving in exactly the wrong direction. With the first peaks of salvation in sight, less than a mile offshore, they were barely treading in one place.

Anna's head finally started to droop. Marcus looked on helplessly, even as he felt his own final sugar-rush of energy fading.

Then he heard Colin's voice. "Uh oh, watch out, folks."

Marcus' adrenaline spiked again, and he looked around quickly, scanning for more sharks, but the surface was empty of tell-tale fins.

But then he saw the patch of drifting bulbs, like pale tulips floating on the surface. There were perhaps a dozen – an entire school of jellyfish, and the tide was hurrying them right on past.

Suddenly, Rodger grabbed his shoulder and let out a scream.

"Oh *Jesus!*"

He thrashed in the water, clawing at his back, and Marcus could see a stripe of tentacle lashed across his back like a whip burn.

"Son of a *bitch*! Oh my GOD, that hurts!"

Rodger's eyes were wide and frightened. "It's not one of those wasps, is it?"

He struggled in the water, pushing away from the group.

"It's not a sea-wasp," Colin was saying, "or you'd already be dead."

Colin reached out, as if to pull Rodger back into the circle, when the water suddenly erupted.

The shark was maybe fifteen feet, and had evidently been circling below, just waiting for one of them to separate.

The jaws caught Rodger in mid-chest as the big white launched its full body clear of the water.

Mona screamed, scrambling blindly, but Colin caught her and pulled her roughly back.

Anna let out a low moan – all the strength she had.

Rodger looked not much bigger than a seal-pup, locked in the steel-trap jaws, as the two-ton fish twisted in the air like a trout, crashing back down into the surf with a second, even bigger splash, and disappearing.

Rodger's body was rag-doll limp. As he was dragged below, Marcus saw his eyes, already empty and dead.

The good news was, he had likely been killed on impact.

Colin pulled the group away.

"Let's go. It's over."

Mona's shrieks subsided into hiccupping sobs. She began to swim obediently, her eyes tearing and red.

There was not even any blood. It had simply taken him and gone. Marcus wondered how long it had been circling, just waiting for one of them to activate that instinctual button.

What might yet lurk, tantalizingly out of sight?

In the wash of water, Marcus became aware that something had slashed him in the face. He wasn't sure if it was the sheer force of the water, or perhaps even a slapping fin.

Then he realized he had caught a flap of torn tentacle across his own face and down his neck. It felt like a whiplash.

"Hold on," Colin said, and used the boat-hook to deftly peel it away.

"That feels like it left a mark," Marcus said.

Colin glanced at the others. Mona cringed. Anna shut her eyes and turned away.

Marcus ran his fingers along the centimeter-wide welt that had sprung up all the way down to his shoulder.

When he touched it, he yelped involuntarily. "Owww... Jesus..."

"It looks great," Colin said. "It'll make a good story for a bar."

Then he nodded back towards the island peaks, which were still frustratingly distant.

"But we've gotta live first."

The current, however, was still actively working against them. Despite their efforts, they were inevitably being pulled past the southern point of the island, back out into the ocean... and whatever came next.

Even if it was a tight cluster of islands, how many miles to the next land mass? Or maybe they would just ride the currents through the strait, threading the isles like a leaf over the rocks in a river.

It seemed ridiculous to die now, Marcus thought. But all the frustration, all the determination, all the anger, was simply nothing against the indomitable momentum of the planet.

The southern point of the island was in sight. They had a spectacular view of cliffs, a cove, waterfalls – and they were sailing right past it.

Marcus had, at that point, officially given up hope.

But then, finally – *finally* – as if only waiting for him to despair, the current changed.

Once it happened, it was like a wave rising up under a surfboard.

At long last, the shoreline was drawing near.

His last reserves of adrenaline firing like moonshine in a jalopy, Marcus kicked for all he was worth.

"Almost there," Colin said.

Mona was panting like an old dog. Anna sobbed openly.

But the ocean had decided to pardon them.

It was early afternoon of their second day, when they finally stumbled up on shore.

CHAPTER 5

The moment he felt solid ground catch beneath his feet, still fifty yards from the beach, Marcus fell nearly limp with relief – and was promptly picked up by a swell, lifting him back up again, reminding him it wasn't over yet.

The water was still chest-deep and it was as if the ocean had suddenly changed its mind – or perhaps awakened from a brief doze, to find the four poor souls it had been playing with like a cat, were actually near to escaping her clutches, and at the last moment, tried to snatch them back.

Marcus felt Colin's hand catch the scruff of his neck, shoving roughly, impatiently. "For Christ's sake! Don't punk out now!"

Mona was gasping as if running with a stitch, her eyes staring fixedly on the beach like a finish line.

Anna's head barely struggled clear of the water, too dehydrated for tears, choking in Cheyne-Stokes sobs.

But then Marcus felt the weight settle onto his feet as the water's grip finally began to slip.

Waves now crashed and pushed at his waist – still nearly knocking him over, as if trying to trip him up and drag him back.

As a group, they staggered up on to the beach. Marcus fell to his knees. Mona crawled until she felt dry sand.

Anna dropped limply like a rag, waves washing past her legs. Colin knelt and picked her up, carrying her to higher ground. He propped her up briefly, so he could check her eyes, even as she blinked for consciousness.

Summoning energy, Marcus crawled over, looking up at Colin as he knelt beside her.

"Is she going to be okay?" he asked helplessly.

Colin didn't answer, instead tapping Anna on the cheek.

"Hang in there, girl," he said. "We've made it. The work's all done."

Anna smiled, squeezing his hand trustingly.

"I'm sorry," she said. "I feel so useless."

"Are you kidding?" he said, "*I'm* sorry. I managed to get us sunk and a man killed."

"You saved us," Anna said, shaking her head, but Colin patted her down.

"You all saved yourselves," he said, raising his voice for the others. "We've made it. Now we just have to find someone to get a chopper out."

He patted Anna's cheek again. "You just chill out and lay on the beach."

Colin stood, and Marcus felt him taking control. Worse, he felt himself waiting for instructions. Mona sat at attention like an obedient bird-dog. Colin shepherded the two of them out of Anna's earshot, his reassuring smile turning serious.

"Listen," he said, "She's badly dehydrated. We need to find some fresh water, get some wood, build a fire." He nodded to the sun, which was cresting into early afternoon, and growing hot.

"Any help might still be the better part of a day away," he said, turning to point over the north-east peaks of the island. "We should be on the south-west end of Banta, which means there's a bay on the north shore. That's where we'll find the commerce."

"There's also," he added, "absolutely nothing in-between. So that means I'm going to have to hoof it. And then I'm going to have to be able to find you again."

He glanced up, checking the sun's position in the sky.

"Build a fire," he said again. "I'll be back within twenty-four hours."

'Wait a minute," Marcus said. "You're leaving? What do you mean build a fire? With two sticks?"

Colin sighed, retrieving his duffel, rooting around until he found a small plastic pouch – inside was a shaving razor, a toothbrush and paste, along with several books of matches.

"Always a good survival tip," he said, stuffing a couple in his pocket and handing the rest to Marcus. They spent the next twenty minutes building a large, smoky fire out of brush and driftwood. The flame was broken and stoked by the wind where it crested around an outcropping of rocks that reached out from the cliffs, splitting the beach nearly to the waterline, creating a semi-protected mini-cove on the south side.

The flame warmed the air in a circular breeze, even as the rocks provided shade from the direct sun. Anna relinquished her spot on the wet sand, for a crook in the lee of the largest boulder, still wet and shivering.

Colin stoked the flames up to a bonfire.

"Keep it smoky with leaves," he instructed. "That'll make it easier to find you again." He nodded at their small pile of wood. "You're going to need to keep it going all night."

Colin took Marcus by the shoulder.

"Seriously. It's hot now, but it'll get cold tonight. You gotta keep her warm. And get her some fluids. You gotta take care of her."

Marcus nodded resolutely.

Colin turned to Mona. "You'll all look after each other?"

Mona glanced sideways at Marcus, but nodded.

Colin tipped them his confident, reassuring grin. "I'll not be long, folks."

With that, he turned and begin hiking up the hill at an energetic pace. With the thick foliage beyond the beach, he was soon out of sight.

Marcus turned to Mona.

The two of them had spent precious few moments alone together – never by choice and with only the most perfunctory civility.

Now Marcus looked at her – disheveled, make-up washed clean, skin and hair two days soaked in the ocean. The dark circles under her eyes were nearly as deep as Anna's – and no doubt his own.

"I'm sorry about Rodger," Marcus ventured.

Mona glanced out at the ocean with a shudder.

"Yeah," she said. "Well, I barely knew him. He was just the latest sponsor, right?"

Marcus colored, as Mona eyed him.

"Yeah," she said. "I heard that one." But then her shoulders slumped. "The thing is, you're not wrong."

She turned away from the water, wrapping her arms as if cold.

"You know what bothers me? Now that we're safe, it's like I don't care that much."

She glanced sideways, testing Marcus' reaction. "I mean I *liked* him – I was with him for six months. We slept together. But..."

Mona stopped, looking frankly back up at Marcus.

"It's like he's ancient history. I've already forgotten. Just like if we'd broken up."

She shook her head.

"I've never *had* a bad break-up," she said, "because I never *gave* a shit. And none of them ever cared a whit right back. I guess when we were out there, and I thought I was going to die, I realized there wasn't even anyone who was going to care I was gone."

Marcus cleared his voice uncomfortably.

"Well," he said, "Anna likes you."

Marcus paused. He almost didn't say it. But at this point, why not?

"In fact," he said, "she likes you better than she likes me. And I think we both know you're still going to be around after I'm long gone."

Marcus shrugged. "So you've got *that* going for ya."

Mona frowned back, perhaps slightly ashamed. Or perhaps their first moment of true empathy since he'd known her.

Fearing they might hug, Marcus deliberately broke the contact.

"We need water," he said neutrally.

Feeling the deliberate break, Mona accepted it with a nod.

"Well," she said, "finding it shouldn't be a problem."

She pointed to where the cliff was bordered by twin waterfalls, cascading down both north and south, into the ocean – easy enough – that was how islands worked.

However...

Marcus glanced back the direction Colin had gone.

"I guess I should have asked how we carry water without a bucket?"

Mona let out a tired sigh. Without reply, she turned and simply continued gathering driftwood for the fire.

"What?" he called after her. "You don't have a bucket, do you?"

Mona kept walking, shaking her head.

Marcus breathed a little sigh of relief – awkward moment of intimacy averted.

Although he still had no idea how he was supposed to carry water.

He looked back to where Anna had fallen into a doze, and found himself reluctant to let her out of sight. Even more, in recent days, he'd learnt to appreciate that she might not be there when he got back.

A quick jaunt, he decided – he had to find where the falls emptied into the ocean – and then what? Find a friggin' palm leaf?

There's your Tarzan, he thought. Challenged by carrying water.

With a final quick glance after Anna, Marcus began to jog up the beach.

CHAPTER 6

Anna shivered despite the heat. The direct sun was unbearably hot, but she felt chilled among the damp rocks. Even with the fire, her arms rippled with goose-flesh.

And she was *so* tired.

She couldn't believe they had really made it. The truth was, she had already resigned herself, she was still not quite ready to trust it.

Perhaps with good reason, because now she was afraid she might die anyway. This *had* to be how it felt.

The strip of coast ran along the edge of thick lush forest – yet here in the midday sun, it seemed strangely empty and dead.

The most prehistoric part of the planet.

Desolate, yet all undaunted, on this desert land enchanted.

Her academic-mind, calling forth the lurid lyric of Poe.

On this home, by horror haunted...

Anna shivered.

She sat herself upright, searching for the others, the mere movement causing pain enough to cry out loud.

Mona was loaded with driftwood. Marcus was scouting further south around the point.

Anna looked up at the intimidatingly primeval, volcanic rock that rose up beyond the grove of trees – the bedrock that formed the island.

It already felt different with Colin gone.

With the cove hooded by cliffs, it didn't just feel remote, it felt isolated – as if the cresting cliffs were more of a wall, locking the peninsula off from the rest of the island.

Already semi-delirious, Anna's imagination wandered.

Colin had been joking about dinosaurs – but only half-joking. She remembered the crocodiles that prowled the beaches back on the mainland.

Then there was what happened to Rodger. How much more of a prehistoric monster did you need?

Eyeing the surf, Anna scooted a few feet further from the water.

Now she was seeing movement in every twitching tree branch.

The tickle of the wind also convincingly mimicked that crawly feeling of being watched.

On cue, the fire cracked loudly with burning sap. Anna shrieked a brief little chirp, her adrenaline wasting valuable calories.

The wind over the surf completely drowned her voice. Neither Mona nor Marcus looked up at her cry.

Embarrassed, she lay back down, shutting her eyes, trying to relax, and really wished Colin were there.

Not that she could tell Marcus that.

Although, Marcus was neither stupid nor unperceptive. He probably knew enough.

Anna realized now she had been a fool to allow this trip to happen. It was selfish of her to let Marcus do this – cruel, even. Dear God, just the debt he'd taken on *alone* – when they both already knew it was over?

They knew each other well enough to know *that*, at least.

What was it going to be like for him now, after surviving all this? To go home and get divorced anyway?

Anna could hear him now, with a wry crook of his jaw – 'we could've just skipped the middle-man'.

She half-smiled, but it faded quickly – because moments of affection lingered on – she always *had* affection for him.

Just not love. Not THE love.

And because she had taken what she thought was the safe route, she was going to break his heart.

She had thought about little else besides dying the last two days. That had the effect of clearing out a lot of extraneous illusions.

Now she looked at her life for what it was and wondered what might reasonably come next.

Despite her education, she was even less-suited for the workforce than Marcus himself, who she had admittedly berated for managing to get an economics degree, bereft of applicable skills.

Divorce was unattractive for other reasons – not the least of which, the practical reality that Marcus couldn't afford her *now*. What made her think becoming an alimony burden would change things?

Unless, of course, she found – to coin Marcus' own phrase – a 'new sponsor'.

Which naturally led her to the option that was being dangled in front of her, for the second time in her life.

Second chances were few and far between, yet it seemed she was being given two at once.

At least one of them was the fact that she was alive and lying on this beach at all.

Was that a sign to not squander the other?

Although, she cautioned, *that* perhaps wasn't so much a second chance as a set-up.

Anna had confided in Mona almost a year ago, that the night before Colin left California, he had proposed. She had also admitted she would have said 'yes', except for the fact that he lived in another country, on the other side of the planet, and he wanted to take her with him.

He had promised adventure. Whether he knew it or not, that had been what had decided her.

This Jane had no intention of being in the jungle to get rescued by Tarzan in the first place. In her world, Tarzan moved to the city and learned to use a fork.

And so, as was her nature, Anna had played it safe. In the years since, she had passed it off as maturity. As she had rationalized to Mona, over wine, it was the difference between fantasy and reality.

"I guess we're different that way," Mona replied. "I'd have gone in a second."

It was in the following months that Mona first suggested she take an adventure. It was not long after that she had first brought up Colin – just an afterthought, mentioning that he did charters.

Anna's ears had perked at his name. She remembered how it had been with them, living side-by-side, while she stayed with Marcus. Very very... comfortable. It was never overt. They never even touched.

She had been amazed to find it no different after all these years.

He still made her feel safe.

She glanced furtively down the beach. Marcus had wandered out of sight. Mona was poking around the outcropping just behind him.

The smoke tickled the hair on her neck again, mimicking that feeling of being watched.

And again, as if on cue, there was a crack.

But this time it came from behind her.

She craned her head, to where the cliff loomed above. As far as she could see, the entire beach was sandwiched by sheer walls.

Anna scanned the rocks just above her head. It had sounded like falling rubble, echoing off the cliffs over the ocean air.

The sound was not repeated.

She patted down a couple of unruly hairs popping up on the back of her neck.

Breathing deliberately, slowly, she lay back down, forcing her body to relax.

Above her, the shadow that had been lurking in the rocks stared down with two blinking eyes.

CHAPTER 7

Colin sputtered profanity as he fought his way through the thick brush. He'd been in heavy jungle many times, but always properly outfitted – like with a machete, or a pair of pants that kept your legs from getting cut to shreds – as opposed to having to scale this sharp rocky cliff, barefoot, in the trouser shorts he'd been sleeping in when his boat went down.

He hadn't been on Banta Island in years, and never from the south. The island itself was barely five miles wide and the bay lay at its southernmost point, about three miles northeast.

Colin had somewhat over-emphasized to the others how close they were to real rescue. He wasn't even aware of a Ranger station on Banta. But he *was* confident that, this time of year, given the abiding weather, the bay would be populated with both fishermen and dive boats.

But their little peninsula was segregated by sheer cliff, and there was no way through except over the top.

It got uncomfortable quick. Besides being steep and jagged, the rocks were *hot*, and the sun's beaming rays were utterly unfiltered by the dry saltwater air.

Colin was very aware they still had a good chance of dying.

Sanctuary lay at a distance; it would take him less than half-an-hour at an easy jog.

Just a few pesky obstacles – like razor-sharp, baking-hot, volcanic rock.

But if he just made the plateau, he should be home free. Once he reached the bay area, he could flag a boat, and hopefully call a chopper. At worst, they should be able to get a boat around to the south shore.

He wasn't worried. People out here helped each other in these situations.

But he had to get there, and a lot of getting there was going to hurt.

Colin would do it. This time it was Anna counting on him. To tell the truth and shame the Devil, Colin was climbing over this scalding, razor-rock for her.

He was not happy leaving her back there with Marcus, who was just as friggin' helpless as he remembered back in college, but there was no choice – *someone* had to find help – and quickly.

She had felt so light in his arms as he'd carried her up the beach.

Then there was that look of trust in her eyes.

Ever meet the perfect girl, perfectly wrong? Star-crossed, they called it.

He had asked her a question once. After she had said 'no' to that question, he had left the States and come home.

Marcus had been his roommate – he hadn't really even liked him that much, so much as adopted him as kind of a pain in the ass sidekick.

It was ironic – Colin had stepped in between Marcus and those footballers that night, so Marcus could go home and bang his dream girl in the next room.

No good deed...

Now here he was again – playing hero.

Truth to tell, he never really felt the part. He was no 'do-gooder' – in fact, he was rather impatient with the characterization. He'd worked a stint as a lifeguard, for example, not because he wanted to guard the public, but because he was a strong swimmer, and it was congenial enough to spend his days at the beach.

Certainly, he had pulled a straggling swimmer or two out of the surf. He had even resuscitated a young boy, and would forever be enshrined by his mother – he still got cards at Christmas.

Truthfully, Colin felt a little embarrassed at the acolytes and frankly, a bit irritated at always having to pull idiots out of the trouble they got themselves into.

It wasn't that he had a problem with *doing* it – he did it because he *could*, and when push came to shove, *someone* had to step up.

But there *was* a little bit of 'why-do-I-gotta-do-*everything*'. It was easy to get impatient with regular people who weren't physically-gifted alphas.

Colin tried to imagine Marcus scaling this cliff.

To his credit, Marcus would have probably tried.

Died trying, but tried.

The crest was finally drawing near. The last stretch, however, was steep. He felt his way, rock by rock, testing his hand-holds carefully lest they pull loose under his weight.

High above, the sun beamed down.

Colin looked back down to the beach. The grove of jungle blocked his view of their little camp, but he could still see the smoky fire.

Marking the spot where he'd left her.

He remembered the last time he'd left her – that one night all those years ago. He hadn't spoken directly to her since – not even a second-hand e-mail through Marcus.

They never discussed her answer to his question.

Likewise, he had never told her – or anyone actually – the *real* reason he'd left that night.

He had just gone home, moving on with the adventures he'd scheduled for his life. He'd gone to work for the Coast Guard, earning rank and medals – before starting his own charter business.

Constant adventure – touring the most prehistoric parts of the planet – where there were not just sharks, but massive five-thousand pound Great

Whites – crocodiles sixteen-feet long – not just snakes but a whole range of seven-step-drop-dead snakes – not just jellyfish but sea-wasps. And to hell with 'killer bees', they had friggin' fist-sized hornets that could drop you dead in twenty-minutes or less.

As he entered the jungle, none of those things were confidence boosters.

He consoled himself that, once you got inland on these little islands, there really weren't any big land predators – no big cats, for example.

Colin had spent time in tiger country – notorious man-eaters – although he'd only had one serious encounter. Their guide had simply faced the big, snarling cat down. It had turned and disappeared, and their little caravan had proceeded on through the brush – with Colin now wondering whether the five-hundred-pound feline might not be circling back.

Fun fact about the genus Panthera – fossil records confirm they've hunted hominids as regular prey since prehistoric times. Contrary to myth, they did not *become* man-eaters, either through injury or having 'tasted human blood' – humans were just another animal, and if you were there and they were hungry, they'd come after you.

But it was different in this part of the world. The big mammalian predators had not yet taken hold.

Looking on it that way, he thought, bolstering himself, he actually held a certain advantage. He was a warm-blooded turbo model, chugging about on a land full of semi-amphibious cold-blooded competitors, still sprawling on their bellies.

In this environment, he thought, nodding with affirmative false-confidence, *he* was the super-predator.

Just so long as he watched the bushes – all those seven-step snakes.

Colin *hated* snakes – the one reptile group specifically evolved to kill mammals, an offshoot of lizards that split off in the Mid-Cretaceous and began chasing mankind's rodent ancestors down their holes.

Of course, the serpents around these parts wouldn't be looking to *eat* him – only bite him if he got too close.

Not that there was a lot of practical difference in how dead he'd be. But there *was* a certain dread at the thought of being *consumed*.

There were only a couple of snakes that could do that to a grown man – the Anaconda among boas, a few species of python – notably the Reticulated Python.

But again, not around here. While the fauna was undeniably dangerous, Colin was at least reassured that there was nothing this far inland that was actually trying to *eat* him.

Kill him, maybe, but not eat him.

Which, of course, would leave his body to be consumed by scavengers, so he supposed you got there anyway.

Taking a breath, moving minimally but efficiently, he made his way through the brush – which he now realized was not a 'plateau' so much as highlands. There was both grassland and trees, which largely blocked his view of the surrounding terrain. He did his best to stick to open fields – except for places where the grass got too tall – as he meandered his path deliberately east.

How far still? By his measure, at least a couple more miles.

But then he realized that the grass was already giving way to bare rock, just like he'd left back on the opposite shore.

Sure enough, as the brush ahead cleared, he found himself staring out at yet another abrupt drop-off, this one a straight drop into the ocean.

Colin frowned. He'd barely gone a mile.

Then a point of greater import dawned.

He now had a good view of the eastern coast going north.

There was no bay. No boats. As near as he could tell, there wasn't even any beach.

He looked down over the drop-off into the ocean. If they had tried to come in on this side of the island, they would have found sheer wall as far as he could see.

The greater import of *that* dawned a moment later.

This wasn't Banta.

Colin blinked, looking up and down the unfamiliar coast.

So where the hell were they?

There were a lot of smaller islands dotting the region, many of them uncharted. Depending on how far the current had taken them, they could be on any one of them.

That changed things a bit.

Colin began walking along the cliffside, heading north to where the bay was *supposed* to be – a proactive motion, while he figured out what to do.

He would scout a little more, he decided. Other islands had ports and fishermen – some even had villages.

He couldn't go back to the beach without finding help. If nothing else, that meant climbing that damned cliff again.

It also changed the situation for Anna. If he couldn't make outside contact, potential rescue might now have gone from hours away to days or more.

The welling anxiety he felt was not for himself.

He stopped, taking another deliberate breath. He was emotionally involved. He knew better.

After a moment, he began a calm walk, cataloging landmarks and distance, as well as keeping an eye on the sun.

The island was obviously smaller than Banta, but he still had to leave himself daylight to get back to the beach if necessary. He didn't want to try the long grass in the dark – that would practically be inviting a snakebite.

And even as he thought it, he caught a rustle in the grass, just at the edge where the foliage thinned, giving way to rocks.

Colin shivered a little – most likely a gust of wind.

Now that he thought about it, he'd actually not seen any snakes.

"Count your blessings," he said aloud, scanning the grass.

The east coast jutted out going north along an ancient volcanic break – apparently, part of the island had once fallen off into the ocean.

As he reached the end of the easternmost fork, he got his first look at the north coast.

The sheer drop along the cliff maintained, bordered by jungle and grassland. The slope led up an elevated plateau.

Mounted like a citadel atop the rocks was what looked, for the life of him, like a medieval castle.

Not that it was made of stone, Colin thought, taking it in – it was *gothic*.

Yet, the closer he got, and he could see more of the building's design, he realized it was, at the same time, obviously quite scientifically modern. He could see antennas and satellite-discs, as well as solar panels, and even a mill, mounted where waterfalls on both sides emptied into the ocean.

Well, there's your human habitation, Colin thought, instantly buoyed. This was no native village – the inhabitant of *that* house would have supplies and a direct link to emergency lines.

He stepped up his pace. The bare rock along the drop-off provided a natural path along the coast – the trees and grass kept respectfully back, where the rich volcanic soil allowed their roots a solid grip – no doubt regularly tattered by tropical wind and rain.

The grass at the edge of the rocky path was tall.

Again, he caught a glimpse of rustling movement, like a lashing whip, over the top of the camouflaging blades.

Rather like a dorsal-fin.

Colin stopped. Something was moving in between the strands.

He did a quick review of what kind of animals lived on these islands.

Goats and pigs had invaded a lot of the local ecosystems. In some places they had completely taken over, eradicating indigenous fauna.

On the mainland, Dingo dogs were similar invaders, but Colin hadn't heard of them on any of the islands.

An animal of any size, this far inland, would have to be a herbivore.

Nonetheless, he stepped up his pace.

A half-mile further on, he found a road cut into the trees – not paved, but manicured and matted down, turning from the cliff inland, evidently leading a path through the brush to the house.

The hollow beckoned, hooded and dark.

Even as behind him, the grass once more began to rustle, and Colin again saw the flash of a snapping whip.

Then the grass parted.

The thing stepped fully out into the open.

Colin blinked as he realized what he was seeing.

Then a low breath.

"Oh *no*."

He knew two things right then – he knew what it was.

He also knew he was in trouble.

CHAPTER 8

Anna had fallen asleep. She wasn't sure what had roused her.

At first, she thought she was coming out of a dream – one of those old 'Lost World' movies that used live lizards on miniature sets, sometimes with rubber fins or horns glued on their heads.

Anna blinked, peering through blurry eyes.

She realized the creature was still there – still coming towards her, running along the beach with its mouth gaping.

Right at her throat!

Anna jerked herself awake with a long lingering scream, just as the jaws clamped shut, snagging her hair, and for one horrifying second, she thought she would be trapped. But the razor teeth sheered through her blond locks like scissors, and she wrenched herself off her back, onto her feet, staggering backwards against the rock.

The thing spat out the mouthful of hair distastefully, again turning in her direction.

A long, snake-like tongue lolled out from between its scaly jaws.

Tasting her on the air.

The thing was nearly ten-feet long and fat as a croc. A huge lizard.

Anna had heard of Komodo dragons. Colin had called these islands prehistoric.

She brought her hand up to where an entire patch of her hair had been sliced away.

The thing was coming towards her again.

It was not hurrying this time, moving in slow and deliberate. As if sensing she was trapped, it actually seemed to pause.

Then she realized, it wasn't reacting to her.

There were two more of the things on top of the rocks behind her.

One of them peered down, less than ten feet above her head, that snake-like tongue reaching down, interestedly.

The greedy leer of the predator – happy to see you, but not in a *good* way.

Anna felt a pulse of horror. Despite her exhaustion, the last lingering fumes of adrenaline sparked, and she sucked breath for a guttural scream.

Her voice barely even seemed to be there, this close to the ocean.

The advancing dragon paid no mind at all, picking its way up the sand, warily eyeing its two competitors on the rocks.

Anna screamed again. *"Help me!"*

But even as the wind drowned her cries, she realized any help that might come would be too late anyway.

If she wanted to live, she was going to have to fight.

She picked up a rock, ignoring the strain in her dehydrated muscles, and with a wild yell, brought it above her head and then down, just as the razor jaws again rushed in.

The rock landed heavily on the big lizard's back – perhaps with a little more force than the creature was expecting, because it let out a startled 'woof', and curled with the impact, slashing its whip-like tail, gaping its jaws and hissing balefully.

Anna looked around for another rock, keeping her eyes on the stalking lizard, even as it eyed her appraisingly. The thing retreated a dozen steps, hovering at the perimeter of the rocky cove. It also kept a close eye on the two usurpers on the rocks – who had yet to make a move, and were most likely simply waiting for the opportunity to freeload off the kill.

The dragon began to plod forward again. Its muscular arms moved hand-over-hand, as it *edged* closer, having learned caution.

Anna reached for the biggest rock she could lift.

As she turned, the dragon made its move – a sudden burst of speed, jaws wide, leaping for her unprotected leg.

Helpless, Anna screamed again, no longer a cry for rescue, so much as a last, agonizing wail of despair – a prey animal run-down, only seconds before the kill.

She stumbled, falling to the ground.

In a flash, the dragon was upon her.

And then suddenly there was a scream to match her own – a wild ape-like howl almost in her ear – and she felt herself shoved roughly aside.

Anna saw the dragon's jaws snap shut just short of her right leg, even as she hit the ground and tumbled.

When she turned, she found the rows of teeth, sheathed by gum-tissue, gaped bare inches from her face, reaching, *straining*.

And holding those teeth at bay, was...

Well, it *looked* like a damned *caveman* – a capering hairy hominid, who actually had the dragon by the tail, corralling it the way Anna had seen experts do with large, venomous snakes and constrictors, turning the thing face-first back towards the surf.

The dragon thrashed and the man released, now advancing with a sharpened stick that he poked aggressively in the creature's face.

The dragon ceded ground, retreating a few steps, before it stopped, panting.

Anna took in her benefactor. The man was wild-eyed and full-bearded – and covered in rags that might have once been jeans and a t-shirt.

As he turned and looked at her, his eyes widened as if with recognition.

Anna, for her part, stared back, stunned motionless with shock.

From above, the two other dragons were now moving down after them.

The caveman again advanced, brandishing the sharpened stick, smacking the first of them smartly across its shoulders and head. The thing ducked, like a dog bracing to be slapped.

Anna faded back as the big lizards advanced in that same slow, deliberate plod.

The caveman grabbed a flaming branch from the fire, waving it in a wide arc. The dragons paused.

There were more of them on the beach. Anna saw at least two or three more poking their heads up among the rocks.

In the final stages of exhaustion and starvation, she actually felt her legs trembling as she tried to stand, stumbling her way past the outcropping, where the surf was starting to encroach with the incoming tide.

She heard an objecting grunt from the caveman – it sounded like "*Hey!*"

When she looked back, she realized yet another dragon had been waiting on the rocks above, and was now making its way down to the sand.

The snake-tongue slithered out, and the slow plod gave way to a fast lope as the thing came after her.

It was smaller than the others, perhaps only seven-feet. But it was faster – and certainly big enough.

Anna turned and tried to run. But the one burst of energy was all she had. The world went suddenly dark and she felt something hitting her abruptly in her chest, knocking out her wind. She realized it was the ground, a half-second before her head smacked into the sand.

She blinked, looking up. The dragon was almost on top of her.

Anna shut her eyes, too tired now to even scream.

But then she heard the caveman ape-cry again.

There was a wet, puncturing sound and an outraged, spitting hiss, but the razor teeth never touched her.

When she opened her eyes, it was to find the dragon had been skewered through the chest with that same hand-cut wooden spear. With a savage, purely animal growl, the man twisted the spear deeper, even as the hundred-pound lizard thrashed like a snake on a spit.

The caveman leaned with his weight, driving the spear-tip through the dragon's body into the sand.

Now some of the creature's fellows were making their way around the rocks.

Anna's vision blurred.

The last thing she saw before she blacked out was the caveman leaning over her.

She felt herself being lifted. His arms were strong, almost cradling, as he began to run, carrying her up the beach.

Now barely semi-conscious, Anna was only vaguely aware she was being taken deeper into the bush.

Then the world dimmed away for a while.

CHAPTER 9

Marcus' jellyfish sting was starting to smart. Out in the hot sun, and the salty air of the beach, the damaged skin began to dry and then burn. Mona had showed him his own swelled-up face in her vanity mirror – he realized only once they hit the beach that she had gone through that entire ordeal with her purse on her arm – and the angry welt divided his face to his shoulder in a straight-line as dark as a smear of lipstick – puffed slightly like a gorged vein.

Mona had snapped her mirror shut sympathetically.

Yeah, Marcus thought, that'll leave a mark. Like the sort that might disfigure his face forever.

He shut his eyes.

Count your blessings. They were lucky to be alive.

That was when he heard Anna scream.

Marcus and Mona exchanged alarmed glances. Their path had taken them just around the bend, just out of sight, but the scream carried over the waves like a squalling seagull.

"Oh my God," Marcus said, starting to move. "Anna..."

And as he did so, there was a flash of movement from the rocks.

Behind him, Mona screamed as something large and scaly darted out like a striking snake.

Marcus looked up just as the razor teeth buried into his leg.

Unreality washed over him as he saw he was now locked in the jaws of a giant lizard.

The thing was as big as he was, and it thrashed and twisted, digging the teeth deep, shredding the skin and muscle clear down his calf.

Marcus let out his own scream, turning to fight.

But the thing had latched on, and Marcus realized if he pulled too hard, it would simply strip the flesh from his entire lower leg.

Given the current circumstances, that would be enough to kill him.

Almost surprised at how calmly he seemed to be reacting, he poked at the lizard's blinking eyes.

The thing made a snake-like hiss, adjusting its grip, eyeing Marcus contemptuously.

But then suddenly Mona was there, careening down with a large rock, thudding heavily on the wide, scaly head.

The dragon hissed again, recoiling, releasing Marcus' leg and gaping its jaws in Mona's direction.

Mona brought her purse whipping down across the scaly face, cursing, spitting, unleashing a fusillade of blows.

Seemingly unhurt, the big lizard nevertheless gave ground, moving up and over the rocks, out of Mona's reach, where it perched, like a crow on a fence post, the tongue sneaking in and out, and simply settled down to wait.

Marcus was holding his bleeding leg. Mona bent down beside him.

"Jesus," she said, somberly, "it got you good, Marcus. It almost severed your tendon."

"I think that's what it was going for," he said.

Mona dumped her demolished purse, pulling out several maxi-pads, and used them to douse his wounds.

"What?" she asked, seeing his expression.

"Nothing." He couldn't wait to tell *this* part of the story.

Behind them, the dragon stared down from its perch, licking Marcus' blood off its lips.

And where there was one, there were others.

As if on cue, another scream drifted down the beach.

"Oh God," Marcus breathed. "Anna..."

CHAPTER 10

The dragon was the biggest Colin had ever seen. He had taken a lot of tours to the dragon islands. Komodo periodically allowed dragon-tourism – a highly-guarded practice where local rangers would allow sightseers past well-fed and presumably non-aggressive dragons.

The big lizards existed on several islands in the chain – mostly considered sanctuaries, as the species was listed as 'vulnerable' due to its extremely localized range.

They were also popular in reptile parks, although they had never been farmed like crocs, because their skin was too tough. Evolved on volcanic islands, dragon scales contained tiny bones called osteoderms, mimicking armored chain-mail.

Besides making them useless for the leather market, it also made them very hard to kill.

Over the years, Colin had seen some damned big dragons, fat and decadent in captivity, many eight and nine feet long. With half of that being tail, that meant a hundred-and-fifty-pound animal. A really monstrous one would approach two-hundred.

Of course, they weren't *all* that big – most dragons actually tended towards coyote or cougar-sized predators.

THIS thing could have squared off against a Siberian tiger.

Monitors were a formidable clade, and somewhat underrated in terms of danger to humans. The low body-count attributed to these big lizards was strictly a product of their isolation. Where monitors had people, they ate them.

They were *mean* too. Three-foot Nile monitors could tear a house cat into confetti. There was at least one case where a number of pet Nile monitors killed and ate their owner, right there in the studio apartment where he kept them.

But Komodo monitors were something else. Their razor-toothed reptilian jaws were only part of the package. They boasted powerful, heavily-clawed forelimbs, that gave up nothing to a comparably-sized leopard, as well as that chain-mail pelt and a cold-blooded, regenerative invulnerability. It could bolt like a lizard, with an improbable endurance that should have been unlikely in an ectothermic animal.

And as a hunter, it didn't even need to fight. It didn't need to wrestle down a buffalo like a tiger. It just moseyed up and bit it on the leg – best choice, the tendon right below the calf – often a crippling wound by itself.

But its real weapon was venom.

Until recently, it was widely-believed dragon-saliva caused bacterial infection, but this was actually a product of the putrid waterholes prey animals often retreated to after being bitten. Dragons, as it turned out, had quite sanitary dental hygiene, often licking their lips with that lolling tongue for several minutes after devouring a meal.

Komodo dragons killed in two ways. Either it simply tore the victim apart right there on the spot or, for larger prey, made a tactical bite, introducing its venom – inducing shock, a drop in blood-pressure, as the anticoagulant toxin caused the animal to bleed out – often within half-an-hour.

Of course, dragons were also known to track prey for days.

Colin knew the stories. Once they got your scent and decided they wanted you, they just followed until they got you.

And *this* thing was looking right *at* him, the forked tongue licking in and out, tasting the air, unerringly following the scent.

But now it could see him.

The head cocked.

For God's sake, Colin thought, it was a MONSTER – nearly the size of a crocodile.

Now it began to move, *scurrying* towards him like a spider racing down a web.

Colin turned and ran.

The thing was gaining quickly, accelerating with lizard-like speed.

Cutting into the brush, Colin leaped for the nearest low-hanging limb and vaulted himself up into the trees.

The dragon came right up the trunk after him, jaws gaping.

Colin scrambled to the upper branches, and then out onto the largest limb.

The branch beneath his feet creaked, and he grabbed the surrounding limbs, trying to brace his weight.

Scaling the tree like a squirrel, the dragon stepped out onto the straining branch after him.

Colin looked down. It was maybe a fifteen-foot drop. Enough to break his leg if he landed wrong.

The branch creaked again, and the dragon stopped, feeling the give.

Its head cocked. The tongue snaked out, like a frog's, as if to shoot out and snatch him.

Colin edged back, but again the branch protested. Both human and lizard froze.

They stared at each other – a stand-off.

The dragon blinked, unperturbed, and Colin realized it was quite content to wait him out.

He couldn't climb past. He again eyeballed the drop, gauging how long it would take the lizard to make it back down.

Based on how fast it had *climbed* the tree, probably in a flash.

And then it would be on him.

Then Colin remembered the matches in his pocket.

Match-flame was no match for dragon skin, but it was all in how you used it.

The branch creaked dangerously as he rooted out a pack – he lit the entire book and it flashed into flame. The dragon blinked, watchful but unbothered, until Colin tossed the fireball into the dried leaves around it.

There was an immediate flare as the branches ignited, followed by an outraged, squealing hiss. Spitting and clawing at the flame, the dragon flipped on the branch, nearly tearing it loose from the tree, retreating back down the trunk in the blink of an eye.

It hit the turf and kept going, disappearing into the brush.

Colin pulled back from the burning leaves. Grabbing a sturdy branch, he hopped off, letting the limb slow his fall until he dangled only a few feet from the ground. He dropped to the forest floor, eyeing the brush warily.

The dragon – seemingly – had disappeared.

How many more of THOSE things were running around?

He did a little retroactive estimate of latitude-longitude. There was a whole series of islands in this chain.

Any one of them within range might well host a whole population of dragons.

It was still the most undisturbed area in the world, inaccessible and inhospitable even when armed with modern technology – let alone barefoot in his skivvies.

He'd called it prehistoric – he liked that. And secretly, he'd always fancied himself a bit of the primitive.

At the moment, however, he was feeling genuinely unnerved in the brush for the first time in his life. Suddenly, he was looking at potential ambush behind every bush. Even small dragons could deliver a dangerous bite.

And once blood was drawn, every dragon in the area would come, following their noses and those long flicking tongues.

They could also, Colin realized, smell infirmity and sickness – if someone was vulnerable and weak.

Like Anna. Colin stopped, staring back the way he had come.

Lord, he wished he hadn't left her.

Colin was doubtful Marcus would be much protection. Certainly not against the thing that had just chased him up a tree.

Although, Colin thought, glancing around, if he didn't get moving, he might wind up with a whole pack of the bastards on his tail. He wouldn't *need* that big one – three or four eight or nine-footers could tear him apart like any hapless goat or cow.

In fact, that big one might have actually *helped* his chances – smaller dragons would surely give a beast like that a respectful breadth.

At least within its range. And Colin wasn't sure how far that extended.

Not that it really mattered. It just became all the more dire that he get help immediately. He stepped back up into a quick dogtrot.

When he'd cut into the forest, he'd lost sight of the castle, but now he broke through the heavier foliage and the building came into view again.

He could also see the sky, as the sun advanced into late afternoon. He had been gone over two hours. He began jogging down the road towards the house.

As he did so, the grass on the side of the road rippled with movement.

CHAPTER 11

Colin paused long enough to spot another dragon looking up over the grass behind him. And then two others.

They were tailing him, and probably had been all along – likely waiting for that big-monster sonofabitch to either make the kill or leave the area. Now that the coast was clear, they were moving in.

Colin glanced around at the brush. There was no telling how many more might be out there – or waiting up ahead.

That question was answered a moment later, by yet another snake-like head popping up by the side of the road.

They were trying to surround him.

Colin picked up his dogtrot a little more.

The castle should be just up ahead. The trees were breaking into a clearing, leading up to the plateau that seemed to be the highest peak of the island.

For the first time, Colin got a clear view of the entire property.

It was bizarre. 'Castle' wasn't right. It was really more evocative of an old temple, ancient and molded into the jungle.

The illusion stemmed from a great deal of effort spent not infringing on any part of the natural fauna – the building was on stilts, mounted over solid volcanic rock, where rainwater pooled, and then ran off the cliffs that surrounded it.

Colin was reminded of an old sci-fi time-travel story, where constructs from the future were built so as not to touch even a single leaf of the prehistoric jungle, lest such invasiveness cause an irrevocable butterfly effect.

He also noted that the building was fortified with imposing spiked rails for fencing.

With his first look at the grounds underneath, Colin could see the reason why.

The volcanic pit below the building was *crawling* with dragons.

In fact, it seemed as if the natural reservoir functioned like a habitat designed specifically just for them.

A habitat, Colin wondered. Like a zoo?

Or more properly, a preserve?

The road led onto a suspension-style bridge that attached directly to the building. The utilitarian lower levels stair-stepped into a round dome, mounted overlooking the ocean. These seemed to be living quarters – and rather swanky at that.

The entire construct stretched across a shallow basin, a natural split in the volcanic rock, where the lizards congregated in its shade.

These, Colin noted, were smaller dragons – mostly five and six-footers.

Except, that is, for one big bastard, perched like a gargoyle on the fence. It wasn't as big as that monster sonofabitch in the woods, but it was still an enormous dragon – easily as large as any monitor he'd seen in any zoo. It presided over its smaller fellows in the pit, ruling the roost like a tom-cat on an alley post.

It seemed to have spotted Colin. The fat forked tongue slithered out of its scaly mouth, licking its chops.

A grim sentry, the big lizard clung casually to the spear-tips, as if in contempt of the sharpened edge.

The spiked gate *was*, however, enough to keep Colin out – at least without effort. When he tested their edge, the fence barbs were plenty sharp.

Experimentally, he banged on the bars.

"HEY!" he called loudly. "Anybody here?"

His voice echoed off the walls of the basin. Colin waited long moments.

Finally, he began looking around for some way to scale the fence. Possibly, he could pad the edges with brush.

But as he turned back, two dragons stepped out onto the path.

The grass rustled and several more dorsal-fin tails thrashed.

Behind him were iron gates.

That big bastard on the fence perked interestedly.

Colin looked up at the sharpened spears – he wasn't going to be given a choice. He jumped up to grasp the spearhead just below the tip, even as the first of the dragons suddenly darted forward, jaws gaping, in a rush at his lower leg.

In a flash, the others followed suit.

They were going to catch him, Colin saw, even as he struggled to pull himself out of reach.

But then he heard an aerosol hissing and felt a gust of air, which he realized was coming from spigots mounted on the fence itself.

Colin felt a chemical sting in his nose and braced himself....

... and then blinked.

Perfume? he thought.

His sailor's nose recognized the scent – *Hot Kitty*?

But the lizards reacted as if it had been pumping tear-gas. They scattered into the brush like a school of fish. Even the big one on the fence slithered down and ducked out of sight into the surrounding greenery.

Behind him, Colin heard a locking mechanism click, and the sound of a motor. Colin let go of the spear-tip and dropped to the ground, as the gate began to slide open.

Even the dragons in the pit had scattered, retreating to the far side of the compound. The decaying meat stench from the basin blended with the cloying perfume, calling up associations with third-world whorehouses and his days in the Navy.

Colin's eyes teared. And as he wiped them clear, he realized there was a man standing on the bridge.

He was an older fellow – white-haired and bearded, beefy rather than portly – and he eyed Colin mildly enough, cutting the image of Santa Claus, retired and living in the islands.

When he spoke, his accent was old-world English.

"Looks like you've got trouble, my friend," he said.

He carried a rifle crooked over one arm. It was not aimed *at* Colin, but it was not exactly aimed *away* from him either.

The man nodded, indicating the gate. "Best come along inside," he said.

Colin glanced back towards the brush to see the first of the dragons were already poking their heads back up over the grass. After a moment, they began to amble back in their direction yet again.

Implacable bastards, weren't they?

There was another spray of aerosol and the dragons paused, but this time they didn't retreat, as if they didn't believe the bluff this time.

Then there came the genuine acid-bite of tear-gas from spigots right at the forest edge, and now the dragons scattered for real, hissing and spitting.

Colin held his nose, eyes already watering, as he turned to the old man, who beckoned urgently to the gate.

"*Inside* please."

Colin followed onto the bridge, while the man stood at point, watching the brush until the gates were completely closed and locked.

Then he turned to Colin, extending his hand formally.

"My name is Burroughs," he said. "Richard Burroughs. This is my home."

CHAPTER 12

Colin took the extended hand, introducing himself as 'Captain' Colin Braddock – late of The Challenger.

"I've got people who need help," he said. "Our boat went down. We've been adrift for two days. There's a woman in a bad way."

He looked back to the brush where the lizards had disappeared, and then down into the pit, where some of them were beginning to wander back.

That big bastard on the fence was back too – just watching.

"And if there's more of those things..." Colin began.

"Oh, there are definitely more," Burroughs said, nodding affirmatively. "Your friends are in very grave danger."

Burroughs turned on his heel. "Come with me, please."

He spoke in the tone of one accustomed to giving orders to staff – and being obeyed – although Colin saw no sign of anyone else.

"Mr. Burroughs," he said, "pardon me, but just what the hell *is* this place? I thought I was on Banta."

Burroughs' brows raised mildly. "About ten miles south, actually. This is my island."

Ten miles? Colin thought. The tide had pulled them *far* astray. With the cloud cover, there had been no way to tell. The current had been well on its way to washing them out to sea.

"You own this island?" Colin asked.

"I do," Burroughs said. "Funded by a foundation from my family. I run a breeding facility for endangered species."

He smiled, nodding to the pit.

"I grow dragons," he said.

Colin sniffed at the perfume still clinging to his shirt. "Is that Hot Kitty?"

Burroughs nodded. "It was my wife's scent."

"A conditioning mechanism?"

Burroughs' brows raised again, approvingly. "Very good, Captain. Yes. Monitor lizards respond very well to behavioral conditioning. Particularly scent conditioning. No sense dousing everyone with tear-gas if you can scatter them with a trained scent."

He smiled. "Sort of an anti-Pavlovian-dog, negative-reinforcement mechanism. You give them a little mace, but before you do, you give them the scent of something else. In this case, perfume. It's a strong scent and it teaches them to avoid it." He shrugged. "Bleach and Lysol both work as well, although neither is particularity comfortable to wear on human skin."

Colin glanced archly back at the brush, and imagined trusting that big-monster-son-of-a-bitch to be driven off by Hot Kitty.

Although, to be fair, he had a few friends who had learned to be.

"Why not just shoot them?"

Burroughs frowned.

"Well," he said, "first of all, because that would defeat the point of this place as a *preserve*, Captain Braddock. For just these endangered animals."

Burroughs turned a reproachful eye.

Colin said nothing. But he didn't look away either. Personally, he had little patience for anyone so over-concerned with an animal of *any* kind, that they would hold back with non-lethals if a person's life were at stake.

Not to be ungrateful.

Burroughs eyed him a moment longer before turning again at a faster pace for the house.

"Besides," he said, "if I had shot one of them, the smell of blood would have stimulated the others."

He shook his head. "Dragons won't scatter from gunfire. They're mostly deaf. And then there's their skin. Buckshot will just piss-off a big one. It might run, or it might come back after you. If you're going to shoot, you need a decent-caliber bullet, and a shot in the head, or dead in the chest.

"No sense," he said. "Deterrent works just as well. Better."

"Well," Colin said, "I guess you're more confident when your ass isn't about to be bitten off."

Burroughs frowned. "The deterrent is better," he repeated, dismissing the point, impatiently, and motioning for Colin to follow as he led them into the main building.

The rear dock attached onto a large warehouse, with an automated roll-up door that cranked-up heavy and slow. The frame was steel, but the panels looked to be made of glass – although it was probably more like some heavy-duty plastic compound. The gears were remarkably silent, as if sacrificing speed to avoid noise-pollution.

The garage was stocked with all-terrain vehicles, from small beach-derbies, and two-wheel motorbikes, to a large four-wheel Jeep.

As they passed, motion-detectors turned cameras in their direction, and the lights in the hallway clicked on.

"They are programmed to activate," Burroughs said, "if they detect anything taller than three feet."

"You mean a person," Colin said. "You live on an island of dragons, and you have your security set to catch people?"

Burroughs smiled. "It's a good thing I did. It's how I knew you were coming up the road. Otherwise, those dragons would have torn you apart.

"Besides," he said, "people are almost always more dangerous. You can never tell what a person might be up to. You *know* what the lizard has in mind."

The old man smiled easily, his rifle still strapped comfortably over one shoulder.

Colin chose not to argue the point, as Burroughs led them up a wide, spiraling staircase, built around one of the building's main struts. The second story looked to be the lab – the lights were dim, and the walls lined with terrariums. If this was a breeding facility, these were likely incubation chambers. Burroughs led them quickly past.

The stairway to the main floor was gated by two heavy security doors, deliberately sequestering the lower levels. Entering the main lobby was like walking into a five-star hotel.

Colin looked around wonderingly. Dome-like high ceiling, chandeliers, with an open stairway leading up to a sub-level that circled the perimeter – obviously living quarters.

And despite the space-age technology, the trappings maintained that sense of Goth – like a cathedral.

"You live here alone?" Colin asked.

"I have work crews, occasionally. Regular cleaning and maintenance. They have quarters. And I will sometimes entertain guests." Burroughs smiled. "Of course, that's not even necessary anymore. It's very difficult to be isolated in a virtual world." He pulled out a fancy-looking I-phone. "Give or take the odd satellite-blackout or sunspot, I have quite an active correspondence. Mostly academic circles."

"You mentioned your wife."

"Late wife, I'm afraid. Five years."

Falling into momentary silence, Burroughs led them around the stairs into the main lobby.

There was a fossil display dominating the center of the room – the skeleton of a giant monitor.

Colin estimated the creature would have been over twenty-feet in life, and maybe four-feet across the back. The jaws were easily the size of a large crocodile's.

A plaque identified the beast as 'Megalania'. And then in smaller print, '*Varanus priscus*', 'prehistoric relative of the modern Komodo Dragon – *Varanus komodoensis*'.

According to the sign, Megalania prowled mainland Australia nearly a million years ago and was likely hunted out by ancient Australians.

Colin was not surprised. It would have been an animal that could not be tolerated around human habitation.

He tried to imagine dealing with a creature like that using just a spear or a club.

The thing's claws were bigger than a tiger's. And it wasn't just big, it was *robust*.

Colin had seen tigers out-wrestle big crocs – primarily because these encounters had occurred on sandbanks, rather than in the water. Even a big croc was not really built to fight on land.

What would *this* animal do to a tiger? He'd seen what four-foot Nile monitors did to house cats.

"I saw one out in the brush that was damn near that big," Colin remarked.

Burroughs crooked his head, as one prone to fact-check.

"I doubt that. I'm certain it *looked* very large while you were confronting it. After all, how big does a two-hundred- and-fifty-pound man look? Then give it a tail and double its length. I'm sure it was very intimidating."

Colin allowed that was so.

But he had seen crocs in zoos – or any number of animals known for indeterminate growth, from pythons to carp – and he knew they got as big as you fed them.

If this was a breeding facility, it was even possible there were growth hormones involved. A lot of outfits used them – mostly legally.

"I've seen a lot of dragons," Colin said, "but I've never seen them *this* size. Certainly not on average. And *damn* sure nothing like that thing in the woods."

The largest dragons on the books were over ten-feet – the heaviest cited at over three-hundred-and-fifty pounds. But even that was deceptive because the dragon had just fed, and a monitor will eat eighty-percent of its bodyweight in a sitting, leaving it engorged, much like a snake. So the animal in question might have had a natural weight of no more than two-hundred-and-eighty pounds.

A big lizard to be sure. But that monster *easily* beat three-hundred pounds – by maybe half-again. And it was obviously hungry. Colin had been semi-facetious about the Megalania comparison, but he still put it at over twelve feet long – a size he would have thought freakish.

If not, that is, for all those other nine and ten footers running around.

That big bastard on the fence was over ten feet, and probably two-hundred pounds. It seemed almost regal, the way it sat perched, heavy in the chest, just like the MGM lion – which, Colin understood, had killed its trainer directly after that famous clip was filmed.

"When I was a child," Burroughs said, admiring the fossilized mount, "there was a spider living outside my window. I used to see insects that got caught in its web. And over that summer, I took to catching grasshoppers and other bugs, and tossing them in that web, watching that spider come running down after it." He nodded. "That thing got *big*."

Colin frowned. "So you're just over-feeding them? What's the point of that? If this is about conservation?"

Burroughs arched an eyebrow. Turning from the mount, he let himself into a utilities closet and pulled a ring of keys off the wall.

"It isn't about over-feeding," Burroughs said, motioning for Colin to follow. "It's about creating idyllic conditions, to maximize returns for the most successful breeding. We are trying to create *advantage* for this species, to bring it back from the brink of extinction. Size is an indicator of health.

"The modern Earth," Burroughs explained, "is rather arid. In days past, indeterminate-growth in predators nearly doubled the size of comparable modern animals. Prehistoric crocs stretched over forty feet."

"But you're letting them run loose?" Colin asked incredulously. "Isn't *that* hell on the ecology?"

Burroughs shrugged. "This is not a natural ecology. It's a preserve. Licensed for the express purpose of breeding endangered species. The physical land is deemed too small to be significant in and of itself.

"So, yes," he said, "I give them the run of the island. The hills were already stocked with invasive goats and pigs. The dragons take care of that. I've actually started importing invasive refugees – pigs and goats gathered by authorities from the surrounding islands – and just let them dump on shore. Very cost effective. And ecologically beneficial."

Colin wondered if *that* was a government-sponsored program.

Just letting stray animals run loose on an island to get eaten by lizards? He wondered how *that* would sell to PETA? He almost snickered.

"That thing in the woods was the size of a saltwater croc," Colin insisted.

"There *are* likely a few alphas out there," Burroughs allowed. "An ideal environment will select for it. There *is* a genetic component, even in indeterminate growth. Some animals are just naturally larger than the rest. In humans, we call them giants."

"Got any that size on the property?"

"No. Once they get too big to handle, I chase them out of the pit into the woods."

"Think that's such a good idea?"

"It's better than keeping a predatory lizard that outweighs you near where you sleep."

That, Colin would agree, was undeniably true. Given those two specific options.

"Besides," Burroughs said, "it's best for any animal to be allowed to exist in its natural habitat."

"But you just told me it's *not* natural," Colin said.

Burroughs smiled thinly. "An argumentative quibble, Captain, of the type I have no patience for. Yes, this is an unnatural preserve, specifically designed to simulate near-perfect conditions in its natural environment. The laws of Darwin have been stacked in their favor. A privilege assigned to endangered species."

"Dragons have been around a while, haven't they?" Colin asked.

"About four-million years," Burroughs said.

"Isn't that about the life-span of most species? I mean ninety-nine-point-nine-percent of all species that ever lived are extinct. Follow that pattern, and sure enough, you've got an animal's range limited to just a few isolated islands."

Burroughs' eyes narrowed. "What exactly is your point, Captain?"

"Just that maybe these animals are simply reaching their evolutionary end. It's the natural order. What exactly are you preserving here?"

Burroughs paused, considering, appearing for a moment offended, but turning quickly back to professorial repose.

"Perhaps, then," he ventured, "I am not so much in harmony with nature, but in defiance of it." The thin smile crooked up on one corner. *"Go not gentle into that good night."*

He turned, leading them back to the stairwell, this time up towards the roof.

Colin realized the Gothic tower that crested the building was actually a landing platform for a small chopper.

Burroughs held up his ring of keys.

"Shall we? It's best to get to your people quickly. This island is extremely dangerous."

Colin eyed the chopper doubtfully. "Really?"

"We can't access the south beach by land," Burroughs said. "And trust me, Captain, time is of the essence."

Cursing beneath his breath, Colin helped Burroughs pull back the tarps.

"You know how to fly this thing, right?" Colin asked as he climbed inside.

Burroughs smiled, pulling on his helmet.

"Done it once or twice. Never without an instructor. I'd rather take the Jeep. But, how hard could it be?"

He cranked the rotors alive.

Colin felt his stomach dip as they lurched into the air.

CHAPTER 13

Marcus and Mona huddled by the fire.

Marcus wasn't doing so good. His leg was quite painful, he felt both nauseous and light-headed, and despite the taped-on feminine-hygiene, the wound continued to bleed.

Anna had been gone when they'd arrived at her little grove of rocks.

There had been one instant, running up on that empty beach, where Marcus had gone completely numb – like getting smacked in the head with a baseball bat – that second after impact, waiting for the pain to hit.

When it finally penetrated, there was a good possibility he would break down on his knees and scream.

Taking advantage of the interlude, his momentarily-detached mind took quiet note of tracks just beyond the dry sand of the little cove – trampled into the wet sediment just around the rocks.

He heard Mona running up behind him.

"Oh my God, Marcus. Where *is* she?"

That threatened the numbness and Marcus felt an impulse to slap her, just to stop her from breaking the spell – don't you dare *say* it!

The ocean was starting to wash away the trail, and Marcus followed the tracks to the far side of the outcropping.

He now saw they had been joined on the other side.

There were Anna's bare feet, looking to be in a stumbling run.

And then larger prints in boots – a man's.

Chasing her?

There were also, Marcus realized, the scrambling, clawed prints of dragons.

And now he saw them, less than a hundred yards up the beach – a group of dragons feeding. They tore and pulled at something human-sized, ripping away bloody pieces striped in red.

Mona let out a choking sob.

"Oh my *God...*"

That broke the numbness. It tore loose from Marcus' throat in an agonized scream of horror, pain and outrage.

On utterly thoughtless impulse, he grabbed up a piece of driftwood, and found himself lurching up the beach, staggering on his lacerated leg like a limping deer, bludgeon in hand.

He was evidently an unimpressive caveman – the lizards didn't even look up – and the dismissal enraged him all the more. With no plan beyond simply clubbing the carrion-eating bastards, he just charged blindly.

Right up until he got close enough to see what they were actually feeding on.

He stumbled to a stop, even as his leg wound again spurted blood.

One of the dragons, apparently catching the scent, looked briefly up from its meal.

They were eating one of their own – another dragon – and while its cannibalizing fellows had torn open its stomach and entrails, Marcus could clearly see what looked like a tree-branch carved into a spear, shoved into the unfortunate creature's chest, pinning it to the sand.

It was not possible Anna had done that.

Nor had she, to Marcus' recollection, been armed with a spear.

Just as abruptly as it raged, his fury was suddenly doused with fresh hope.

Mona pulled at his shirt, pointing at the sand.

There were more tracks. The man's prints – alone, this time, but deeper. As if carrying someone.

The tracks disappeared into the dry sand, heading up into the rocks.

Marcus' head was a dizzying whirl. There was the heady rush of relief – Anna was alive – but now that fear was immediately replaced by a new terror.

What was *happening* to her?

"Someone took her," Marcus said aloud, as if to make it real.

He started to follow the tracks up into the rocks, leaving blood in his steps.

Mona caught his shoulder, shaking her head.

"You can't, Marcus," she said sympathetically. "You *can't*."

As if to emphasize the point, Marcus stumbled on his lame leg.

The movement caught the attention of the dragon that had looked up before. Now a second, popped up its head and stared in their direction.

Marcus looked at Mona helplessly.

"We have to wait for Colin," she said, pulling at his hand.

They retreated back past the rocks and spent the next hour gathering firewood. Periodically, Mona would scout with a burning branch up the beach in both directions.

The cove was narrow – it was either wait it out on the sand, or retreat into the grove of trees. On the beach, they could at least see the things coming.

Sure enough, after about an hour – evidently having finished off their unfortunate fellow – the dragons began to gather along the perimeter – some poking around the outcropping, others prowling the rocks above like crows on a phone line, staring down interestedly at their next potential meal. Still others crashed the party late, wandering up from the south beach.

The largest of them were swelled fat, engorged like pythons, having taken the lion's share.

Still weren't full, though.

For the moment, they were taking a break between courses, relaxing along the beach and rocks, belching and licking their lips.

But as a group, their eyes never wavered. Marcus knew all it was going to take was the first of them to get up and start ambling in their direction.

Then the others would start to follow.

Marcus hobbled. They would take him first.

That might at least give Mona chance to get away – but to where? Colin would be bringing rescue back *here*.

Not to mention being *Mona's* martyring-hero wasn't exactly the way he'd dreamed of going out.

As if roused by his thoughts, the first of the big lizards stirred, rising up on its haunches, tongue flicking.

"If they get me," Marcus said, "you run. Find Anna."

Mona actually barked a chirp of laughter as she looked around at the surrounding lizards.

"You're a nice guy, Marcus. But you're kind of a low-rent hero."

Amazing, Marcus thought. She just made getting eaten worse.

A second dragon rose lazily to its feet.

Marcus felt Mona's hand clench on his arm, even as she set her feet, ready to fight. Over one shoulder, she still carried her demolished purse. In her other hand, she held a burning piece of driftwood.

Then, almost as one, the dragons suddenly broke ranks into a skittering sprint, the flock of them bolting like a rabble of squirrels.

Mona shrieked, but the dragons weren't attacking. Instead, they disappeared into the rocks and surrounding brush.

Over the crack of the fire and crash of the ocean, Marcus now heard the chop and wind-blast of rotor blades.

Like a swooping hawk, a helicopter circled haphazardly over the narrow beach.

Mona dropped to her knees, hugging Marcus in relief, nearly burning him with the torch. "Oh thank God!"

The chopper made a couple of attempts at a rather rough-looking landing on the wet sand, and before the rotors even stopped, Marcus saw Colin jump from the passenger side.

He was joined a moment later by an older gentleman, who ambled towards them easily, a rifle strapped across one shoulder.

"They know the chopper," the man was saying. "They won't try the area for a little while. We'd best hurry, though."

Colin took quick stock of Marcus' leg – grimacing briefly, before slapping Marcus on the shoulder.

"It's fine," he said.

He looked around. "Where's Anna?"

With Marcus hobbling, Mona led them back past the outcropping where the tracks disappeared into the hills.

The dead dragon carcass was gone. Limbs and claws had been swallowed whole, with the rest torn into bite-sized chunks. The entire carcass was consumed. Whatever was left, the ocean had already taken.

Colin had called the old gentleman – Burroughs – to inspect the remaining tracks, where the trail disappeared into the rocks.

"Someone was carrying her," Colin said. "Who else could be on this island?"

Frowning up at the surrounding highlands, Burroughs turned heel and motioned them back to the chopper.

"I might have some idea," he said. "For the immediate moment, we need to get your friend some medical attention."

"We need to find Anna," Colin said.

"Then we still have to go back," Burroughs said. "The chopper's no good over the center of the island. There's too much cover. We have to take the Jeep. "

Colin eyed Burroughs steadily.

"Who else is with us on this island, Mr. Burroughs?"

Burroughs looked grimly at the rocks above.

"The man," he said, "who killed my wife."

CHAPTER 14

Anna came awake to find the caveman sitting and watching her.

She sat up abruptly, reflexively pushing back and away, before realizing she was up against a rock wall.

The caveman didn't move, just eyed her. Anna pulled her legs up close to her chest, throwing off the little pile of blankets as she looked around the little hovel – a shallow cave with a makeshift gate of cut branches braced across the entrance.

The primitive nest showed the habits of the occupant – surprisingly organized, with piles of wood segregated from bottles filled with water and cans of food – as well as a handy pile of what looked like hand-crafted clubs and spears.

Anna eyed her host warily – the matted, shaggy hair and beard, the crack-cocaine circles under the eyes.

Now he reached for a small metal box marked 'first aid' and opened the lid.

"Who are you?" Anna asked. "Where am I?"

"My name's Taylor," he said, as he rummaged through the box. "George."

He nodded to the pile of blankets he'd set up for her. "I don't think it's best you move around right now. They're already sniffing around outside. I've been using a lot of deterrents – my own supplies – but they can smell you've got a fever."

"Where am I?" Anna asked again.

Taylor turned, waving a hand at the hollow little hole in the rock.

"Home sweet home," he said. His lips cracked in an attempt at a wry smile, and Anna could see just a little too much white traced around his eyes.

"Did you bring me here?" Anna asked.

Taylor nodded. "You're lucky to be alive."

Now he pulled a large syringe from the box – the sort used on livestock, with a needle as thick as a pencil lead. He poked the tip into a vial of clear liquid.

"What exactly is *that* for?" Anna asked. "Do you use it on a horse?"

Taylor drew the plunger.

"Lizards, actually," he said.

"Are you a doctor?" Anna asked doubtfully.

"Veterinarian," Taylor said. "Well, more of an animal-medic."

He made another effort at a smile.

"A dragon keeper," he said.

He held up the syringe. "That's why you gotta have a big needle. To get it through their tough skin." He cleared the bubbles, popping a small squirt of liquid. "You don't have any allergies, do you?"

Now he turned, eyeing her meaningfully, the needle poised, finger on the plunger.

"*Oh* no," Anna said, pushing back against the wall. "I don't think so."

Taylor sighed. And with the resigned moves of one who has jettisoned all non-essentials – particularity in regards to patience – he simply reached out and grabbed her by the arm, throwing her bodily across his knee in the manner of administering a spanking.

"*Hey!*" Anna squawked, starting to struggle. "Let me go!"

Her bikini briefs exposed a nice fleshy butt-cheek, and she let out an outraged squeal as he poked it with the needle, and held her kicking, hundred-and-forty-pounds still while he pressed the plunger.

"And you know what," he said musingly, "a shot of B12 couldn't hurt either." He drew another dose out of a second vial.

"Here," he said, "one for the other cheek."

Right side this time. Anna shrieked again.

"Nice cheeks, by the way," Taylor said, and let her go.

Cursing, she scrambled back against the cave wall, glaring balefully, her hands rubbing her punctured glutes.

"*Bastard!*"

Taylor shrugged, methodically replacing the vials and needle back in their case. "So I've been told," he said. "You understand, I'm trying to save your life."

Anna blinked as she suddenly remembered the others. If the dragons had come after her...?

"Where are my friends?" she asked. "My husband?"

Colin had been gone – that left Mona and Marcus alone. If there were more of those things, what could *Marcus* do?

"Well, ma'am," Taylor said, his too-wide eyes seeming not to blink, "near as I can tell, Mr. Burroughs has them. I heard his chopper. My guess is he was picking them up. He flew right overhead."

"Why didn't you wave them down?" Anna said.

Taylor chirped bitter laughter. "Let's just say, Mr. Burroughs and I have history."

"And who exactly is Burroughs?"

"Richard Burroughs," Taylor said, "*Doctor* Richard Burroughs, is my former employer and the owner of this island."

Taylor eyed her seriously, still not blinking, showing off the odd eye-tick.

"He's been trying to kill me for years."

Anna absorbed this silently.

"So...," she ventured, "what now?"

"Well," Taylor replied, "that's what I'm trying to figure out."

Now his saucer-eyes actually did begin to blink, like a computer-screen working data.

"I guess it depends," he said, nodding as he spoke. "I figure once they're all at the castle, they'll probably be wanting to call for help."

He shook his shaggy head. "That's what I was waiting on. I figured your friend would find the house. They'd have to send a chopper."

"You were watching us?"

"I saw you land." He indicated the entrance. "We're right on the edge of the cliff. I can see the beach."

He let out a craggy sigh.

"I *was* kind of hoping to maybe get rescued myself."

He eyed her archly.

"But those dragons went for you, so I had to jump in."

He frowned. "Unfortunately, that complicates things a bit."

Anna shifted nervously. "What does that mean?"

"Well," he said regretfully, "now you've *seen* me."

Anna blinked, not liking the sound of that.

"What does it matter?"

"If I let you go, Burroughs will know I'm still out here. And where I've been hiding."

"So, you'd just keep me here?"

Taylor appeared to consider. "Well, I need a mate."

He looked at her deadpan, as every muscle in Anna's body stiffened.

"What?" he said, blinking his too-wide eyes. "No laugh?"

He shrugged. "Sorry. My social skills are a little rusty."

Anna glared. "Not for a Neanderthal," she said.

"You know," Taylor said, frowning, "I *did* just save your tush from a bunch of man-eating lizards. Time was, a woman would be grateful for that. You should be glad I'm a gentleman."

With an ape-like grunt, he heaved himself to his feet, turning to the barricaded entrance. With another grumbling snort, he moved the bracing rocks and pushed the makeshift gateway aside.

The cave opened up onto a modest ledge nestled into the rocks, overlooking the ocean.

Circumstances notwithstanding, it really was a spectacular view – the kind you usually had to pay for.

Taylor stood at the precipice looking down at the beach – a clear vantage to where they had landed. Anna could still see the remnant smoke of their campfire. Taylor was muttering aloud, but now seemed to be talking more to himself than her.

"The problem is that they still have to look for her."

He nodded as if in response to a conversation in his own head. His eyes were sketchy and thoughtful.

"Might be better," he said. "You can't move for a while yet, anyway. It might be better to just stay here and let the *real* rescue party find us."

Anna realized he was talking to her again. "What about my friends?"

"They're safe enough," he said. "Only safe place on the island."

"But you said this Burroughs-person was trying to kill you."

Taylor nodded. "Yes, *me* – but I gave him a reason."

Anna did not doubt that was true. She did not, however, find it particularly reassuring.

"The compound's a secure, modern facility," Taylor said. "About two-and-a-half-miles northeast."

He turned back, smiling with his eyes too wide.

"Keep your enemies closer," he said.

Even as he spoke, Anna heard a knocking sound.

Taylor had fortified the ridge – rather impressively, in fact. Above the cave was sheer wall to the top of the plateau, but the landscaping to either side was stair-stepped slabs of rock. Taylor had blocked access routes with fencing, braced with boulders – more elaborate versions of the makeshift gateway that served as a door to the cave. These barricades were further fortified with sharp-cut branches, and twisted vines roped like netting.

The knocking sound was the top branch in the main gate being broken.

When they turned, there was a snake-like head poking up over the top. An inquisitive tongue slithered between leather jaws.

Taylor stood, brows folding sternly.

"Can't have that," he said. "We've got rules here."

He already carried a forked stick – obviously just out of habit – but now he grabbed up a small plastic squirt-bottle.

Moving as one about to spray a spider, Taylor promptly marched over to the intrusive lizard, and pumped a stream of liquid straight into its eyes.

Komodo dragons have no real voice, limited to hissing like their snake-relatives – but this was as horrible a 'hiss' as Anna had ever heard – deep-throated and ragged.

The dragon twisted off the fence, launching itself back down into the rocks.

Taylor squirted a few more dashes around the fence, even as he immediately set about repairing the post.

Anna caught the scent of bleach.

"Deterrent," Taylor said. "They don't much like it in the eyes. That lizard will be following his nose and not much else for a while. And he'll damn-well stay away from here."

He shook his head sternly.

"Can't be patient. It's conditioning. Spare the rod."

He was talking to himself again, Anna realized, even as he rocked himself just a little. She'd seen monkeys raised in cages do that, separated at birth from their mothers, mimicking the cradling motion – a seemingly universal method of comfort, pantomimed by this scraggly, wild-eyed caveman.

"Can't ever let your guard down with these bastards," he muttered, furtively scanning the perimeter. He gave the patched fence an experimental shake.

"They just sidle up on you," he said.

Taylor picked up the broken pieces of fence, immediately re-purposing them in the corner woodpile, checking the other barricades like a man making daily rounds. Satisfied the gates were secure, he sat back down beside her.

"You know," he said, "at one time I loved them. Dragons were my 'great interest'."

He seemed bitter at the thought.

"*Now*, I pretty much hate them. But I remember all the reasons I was so impressed. Because they have hunted me every single second I've been loose on this island."

Anna nodded. It wasn't as if she wondered *how* the wild-eyes and dark circles had gotten there.

Although she did have a question or two about which came first.

Taylor was talking – again, Anna wasn't quite sure if it was to her or just aloud.

"But they protect me too," he said, acknowledging a fair-point. "They eat all the cobras. Otherwise, you wouldn't be able to live on the rocks.

"And," Taylor said, "they've kept Burroughs from finding me."

Now he turned, speaking to Anna directly.

"He tried to track me down with dogs. You know that? But the dragons ate them. Right down to their collars. The whole damn kennel."

Taylor actually seemed to tear-up for a second.

"You know, I raised most of those dogs."

Then he caught the look on Anna's face.

"No," he said, agreeably. "No, I'm NOT quite stable anymore."

He nodded to his surroundings. "What can I say? I'm a product of my environment. It gets to you after a while."

Anna nodded. She'd been here less than a day, and she could safely say it was getting to her already.

"So, what now?" she asked.

"We wait for your friends. Or more specifically, we wait for a rescue chopper to come for them. And when they do, I'll flag them down."

"So you're just going to keep me here?"

"Unless you feel like walking to the compound." Taylor pointed. "Northeast. Two-and-a-half miles."

Anna subsided.

"Maybe tomorrow," she grumbled, turning away.

"And on that note," Taylor said, reaching for another carrying case, this time producing what looked like a large tin of perfume. "Since you're spending the night..."

With the same purposeful look he had given her when he had poked a needle into her butt-cheek, he turned with the plunger in hand. Without formality, he began to douse her from head to toe.

"Hey!" Anna protested. "What the hell are you doing?"

Hot Kitty? she thought.

"Just getting you ready for your wedding night," he said.

Anna went rigid, tensing, ready to push away.

Taylor shrugged. "Still not funny?"

Anna glared.

"Deterrent," he explained. "Dragons are scent-oriented. We'd release certain chemical scents before we did something unpleasant – like tear-gassing them or turning up the heat-lamps under the building. They learn to associate that smell with pain and they run away. Simple cause and effect."

"Why perfume?"

Taylor's eyes blinked briefly away.

"It's what his wife wore. Burroughs' wife."

Taylor glanced compulsively over his shoulder in the direction of the unseen castle as if it were a clock on the wall.

But this time, the wild white seemed to soften from his eyes.

"It was an extra safety mechanism. With her living here on the island, we figured it would keep them naturally opposed to going after her, if there were ever an accident."

"And did it work?"

Taylor added several more squirts.

"No," he said. "In point of fact, it didn't. But it's a deterrent, not a fail-safe."

He set the bottle carefully back in its box.

His manner seemed to have abruptly changed. The wide-eyed, unabashed stare had given way to skittish self-consciousness.

Mood swings, Anna supposed. Fair enough – crazy people did that.

"You look like her," he said.

"Who?"

"Lorena. Burroughs' wife. You look like her."

And *that*, Anna thought, was the look in his eyes.

He'd said he'd given this Burroughs a reason to kill him. What better reason than his wife?

A wife for whom a dragon 'deterrent' apparently didn't work.

Taylor was looking at her steadily.

Anna wondered what he was seeing.

CHAPTER 15

Taylor set up their little bunker for the night.

He folded the ratty twist of blankets into a semi-padded nest where he directed Anna to lie down.

She eyed him warily. "You're not expecting me to..."

"*I'll* be staying up tonight," he said, cutting her off impatiently. He waved at the surrounding rocks.

"They're out there," he said. "You just can't see 'em yet. They can smell your sickness. They're going to keep coming no matter how much Hot Kitty I squirt you with."

He tapped his pronged stick on the rocks.

"Someone has to fight them off."

When the sun went down, he barricaded her inside, bracing the gate with boulders.

She was, for all practical purposes, now trapped.

Taylor lit a fire, and then simply sat down to wait, poking the embers with his stick.

He had gone quiet, and when Anna had started to speak, he shushed her, as his ears perked for every stray bump in the night.

Once the sun went down, there were a lot of bumps. The island was tropical, the hooting birds alone let out the most blood-chilling screeches you ever heard – and that was just a friggin' parrot.

The things that *really* wanted to get you made barely any sound at all.

They just sidled up in the dark.

Periodically, Taylor would rise to check each gate, waving a burning branch in each direction – adding a squirt of bleach as he did so.

He also fed the fire, poking its embers with the practice of a stone-aged primitive.

Anna found herself listening in the dark as well.

Her fever broke sometime during the night.

She didn't know when, but she must have slept because she had wild dreams.

It was somewhere in that early twilight where it really began – those post-midnight hours of early morning, where the dark began to give up the sway, and the sky sparked like fireflies with the first tints of red.

At one point, she had woken – and maybe was delirious, because she remembered Taylor leaning above her, blending into her fever-dream, and her slapping and clawing at his face.

Impatiently, he held her down, dowsing her face with water and pushing an aspirin between her lips.

He also rolled her over and gave her another shot – first butt-cheek again – but this time she was too groggy to overtly resist. This sting was immediately followed by a kaleidoscopic head-rush, and from then on, she just watched the dream unfold.

It seemed to really begin with the first sparks of the dawning light – the rite of spring – as the unseen bumps in the night gave way to the first-glimpsed reptilian monsters, that had prowled just beyond the firelight, now emerging from the slowly-retreating shadows.

"They like the twilight-zone," Taylor said. "The earliest light, before the heat of the sun."

The dragons did indeed seem to be growing increasingly bold. Taylor tossed burning branches whenever they pressed too close. Several times, he was up, poking through the fence with his stick.

He was also a dead-shot with his squirt-bottle full of bleach. Any inquisitive snouts poking over the fence posts got a nice dose in the eyes – no exceptions. It worked well, and also seemed to scatter the others.

One aggressive individual required sterner measures – a big one, over ten-feet, that looked irritably at Taylor's prodding stick as it perched atop the barricade.

For this cheeky affront, Taylor produced a second nozzle-gun – this one filled with gasoline – and likewise doused the lizard face-first. He then torched it off with the end of his burning stick.

Even in her dream-state, Anna shrank back at the flash of flame.

There was an outraged, ragged hiss, and the crumble of broken boards as the dragon thrashed and bolted, the clinging flame lighting its flight as it disappeared up into the rocks.

Taylor immediately bent to repair the damage to the fence.

How long, Anna wondered, had this routine been going on? Every night for *five years*?

She imagined you'd get a bit sleep-deprived after a while – a little extra white in the eyes.

Anna also began to understand what she was seeing in the slow, careful way Taylor moved.

It was predator/prey symbiosis – prey reflecting the tactics of the predator – shields to claws, horns to teeth, movement to counter movement – becoming a mirror of the predator itself. If you're being chased by a cheetah, you get fast.

But *this* was a war of attrition – slow, deliberate chess – stealthy movement in the dark.

The stand-off between the stalking dragons and her hairy Saint George seemed to endure for hours, well approaching dawn.

But when Anna saw those first full rays of light – the post-school-bell morning sun – the steady, ambling assault seemed to have abruptly stopped.

By the time the sun had risen fully out of the ocean, still droopy and red, it had been nearly thirty-minutes since anything had encroached on the clearing.

Taylor still sat sentry, his stick and squirt-bottle ready. Every now and again, he poked another log in the fire, always making sure he had something suitable as a club in reach, with one end burning.

In a bizarre way, within the strict confines of current circumstance, Anna realized she actually felt very secure under his watch.

Sometime after that, in the still-cool dawn, she finally slept.

CHAPTER 16

At Colin's insistence, Burroughs had taken the chopper up and down the coast before circling back to the house.

Near the rocks at the far end of the south beach, they discovered what was left of Rodger Vaughn washed up on shore.

They scattered another group of scavenging dragons as Burroughs brought the chopper in low enough to have a look.

"There's no place to land," he said. "Is it your friend?"

Mona turned away. Her voice caught as she fought the impulse to gag.

"That's Rodger," she said.

Rodger's carcass stared up at them, waving lazily in the surf. He was gone from mid-torso down, and minus his left arm – the shark had done that. The dragons had hollowed out his chest cavity. But his head was mostly untouched – just a bit pallid and white after a day floating at sea.

Marcus was sure there would be worms and crabs if they were to look a little closer.

Burroughs pulled the chopper back up.

"We can retrieve him by boat," he said apologetically.

"Not a priority," Colin said grimly. "He's dead. Anna's somewhere out there alive."

In either case, Marcus was ready to get out of the chopper, which wobbled like a wounded crow with Burroughs at the helm. His leg was still bleeding, seeping through the taped-on maxi-pads, and the vertigo was getting worse.

Burroughs took one last loop up over the rocks – enough to convince Colin further air-search would be pointless, before circling back to what Burroughs called the 'facility'.

It was bizarre to see the place from the air. The round, dome-like upper level was rather reminiscent of the Starship Enterprise. The penthouse-style upper-deck boasted an Olympic pool on a veranda built right on the edge of the cliff, overlooking the ocean at the north peak of the island – a sunrise/sunset view in both directions.

But as they hovered, Marcus could now see the rest of the compound – the utilitarian underbelly.

They also saw what lurked below.

The dragons in the pit scattered under the house at the sight of the helicopter.

"Jesus," Mona breathed. "What *is* this place?"

"Home sweet home," Burroughs said.

There was a double thump as the chopper's struts hit the tarmac in a rough one-two sequence.

Marcus' stomach nearly revolted. It was physical exertion to hold it back, and the effort actually left him light-headed. He must have tottered, because Mona's hands were suddenly holding him up.

"Marcus? Are you okay? Oh my God, *Marcus*?"

And then for some reason, her voice seemed to fade.

He had a vague sensation of spinning and for a few brief moments, the world went dark.

Although, it must have been a little more than that, because when he blinked back, he was lying in what looked like a small infirmary bed, with everyone standing around him.

Burroughs was wearing a lab coat and tending to the IV Marcus saw sticking out of his arm.

Seeing him awake, Burroughs shined a light in his eyes.

"How are you feeling, Mr... Miller, was it? It's fortunate we didn't tarry much longer getting you back here. You would have likely bled out within the hour."

"How long was I unconscious?" Marcus asked, wide-eyed.

Had it really been that close? That moment of falling – that spinning into the dark...

Well, that had been him dying, hadn't it?

But for a couple of plastic bags of saline and plasma.

He looked down at his leg and saw it was now bandaged more thoroughly. He ran his hand over the wrapping, and realized his leg was numb – local anesthetic – and he could feel the nub of stitches.

"You've been unconscious over an hour, Mr. Miller." Burroughs smiled stiffly, as one unaccustomed to bedside manner. "Your friends have been quite worried."

To their credit, Anna and Colin both looked appropriately concerned.

Burroughs continued his professional review. "You've lost a decent amount of blood. But you're sutured up – seventy stitches. They had to be small and close together, accounting for the anticoagulants in dragon bites. I've administered steroids locally. You're going to need to not move that leg, or you'll tear open again.

"It would also be prudent," he continued, "to get you to a real hospital, and an actual doctor."

"You said *you* were a Doctor," Mona objected.

"*Doctorate*," Burroughs said. "Not a medical doctor." He nodded to the infirmary. "This is just stuff I picked up from reading. First aid and safety protocol around 'hot-herps'. I can also administer anti-venom. Field-medic training is just sort of a survival skill in my line of interest. Sort of like being proficient in CPR when you have an enthusiasm for scuba-diving."

Marcus looked unhappily down at the jury-rigged patchwork of his leg.

It would have to do. Right at the moment, there were other priorities. "What about Anna?"

Burroughs exchanged a grim look with Colin.

"She's... safe. So far as we know..."

Colin glared. Burroughs sighed.

"She's with a man," he said, "who I had actually presumed long dead."

CHAPTER 17

"I had a wife. Her name was Lorena. She's been gone five years now. An accident, if you want to call it that."

Burroughs looked down at his hand, which still bore a ring.

"George Taylor was an employee of mine, back when I kept on-site staff. He was my caretaker – my dragon-keeper."

Burroughs put his hand in his pocket.

"He also had an... infatuation with my wife. Who, to be fair, was probably not entirely innocent."

As he spoke, Colin caught the old man's eyes tip in his direction. Knowingly?

"These are primal matters," Burroughs said. "And they tend to get solved in primal ways. In the case of Mr. Taylor, it was pretty simple. One night, he tried to force the issue."

Burroughs' professorial tone never wavered, but there was a sting of acrimony, tearing old wounds.

"It was all very dramatic, declaring his love out on the back veranda over the ocean, right at sunset. Just as *I* did, in fact."

Burroughs sighed, deep and resigned.

"I'm... not entirely sure what went on with them. I don't even know if she was truly... physically... unfaithful. But I knew there was *something* there, and I had decided to confront them about it.

"Unfortunately," he said, "I was just a little bit too late."

Burroughs frowned, his St. Nicholas face souring, angry and bitter.

"Although, I suppose there would have been little I could have done. After all, he's the rugged young dragon-wrangler and I'm just a doddering old man."

Now he paused, reviewing the memory, not for the first time or the thousandth – speculating, judging, one more time.

"But we'll never know," Burroughs said, "because I *was* too late. She went over the edge. A fifty-foot drop. And she landed in the pit."

For the first time, the old gentleman's relentless methodical movement came to a complete stop – the past claiming his full attention.

"I tried to intercede, but he struck me. And while I was incapacitated, he went over the railing himself. When I recovered, I looked over after him.

"I could see Lorena," he said, "below..."

Burroughs broke off, the memory too vivid.

It didn't matter – by now, they all had a good idea of what he would have seen.

"Mr. Taylor," Burroughs continued, "disappeared into the brush. In the following days and weeks, I made any number of attempts to find him. I even sent staff out with his dogs, figuring they would know his scent. That backfired badly. The dragons went right after them. We lost every one of them to a pup. We barely found an uneaten collar.

"I only assumed," he said, "that Mr. Taylor had befallen the same fate."

Burroughs resumed his puttering, finishing his clean-up.

"Afterwards, I moved all staff off the island, except for periodic maintenance. There's no real need, so long as I do my rounds. The house and the grounds are under almost complete automation. The power is self-sustaining.

"And as it happens," he said, "these days I mostly prefer to be alone. And until just today, I thought I was."

Marcus had sat, absorbing the story through painkillers, and the pertinent implications hit him by degrees.

"So you're telling me," he said, "that this guy has been running loose on this island for five years?"

"It seems so."

"And *this* is the guy who ran off with my wife?"

Marcus attempted to sit up, pulling painfully at his leg. "And you want to just leave her out overnight?"

"She's with a dragon-handler," Burroughs said. "Competent enough to survive this long. He should be able to last another night."

"I'm not worried about *him*," Marcus said. "I'm worried what he might do to *her*."

Burroughs exchanged a brief glance with Colin, who nodded reluctantly.

"I'm afraid we've lost too much daylight," Burroughs said. "The Captain and I are in agreement that tracking her would be prohibitively difficult and dangerous at night.

"And whatever he grabbed her for," he finished, "it wasn't to kill her."

Marcus stared back in outraged silence.

"But what about the authorities?" Mona protested. "I mean, we're rescued now, right? We're plugged back into civilization. Can't we get a search chopper out from the Coast Guard or something?"

"Unfortunately," Burroughs said, "we happen to be on an isolated island in the middle of the Flores Sea. And while modern technology is indeed remarkable, the sun does rise and set, and the Earth does spin on its axis. These and other things will occasionally damp out areas where communications are dependent upon satellites – and can be down for hours or days. We are currently in the second day of one of these extended black-outs.

"But I assure you," he said, holding up his phone "I have an emergency alert set on stand-by, and will auto-call for help as soon as communications are back up."

"Don't you have some kind of back-up?" Colin asked.

Burroughs shrugged. "Morse Code? Short-wave radio? I have them in the shop. Be my guest."

Colin grumbled.

Burroughs looked at them all sympathetically. "I understand you're concerned about Mrs. Miller. If we haven't got outside contact by morning, we'll take the Jeep. Now that Mr. Taylor has popped up, I've got a good idea of where he must have been hiding all along."

Mona looked doubtful. "If this guy's dangerous, won't you need the police?"

Colin's voice was quiet, unassuming, and cold as ice.

"I'm on that," he said.

"Well, then," Burroughs said, turning to Colin and Mona, "if Mr. Miller is comfortable enough, shall we get you acquainted with the safe areas of the property, and set you up with lodgings?"

The circle of unhappy faces stared back. Burroughs held up his phone.

"It's in the lap of the Gods, now," he said. "There's nothing more we can do tonight."

CHAPTER 18

"You live here alone?" Mona asked, as Burroughs led her and Colin down the hall.

She glanced around uncomfortably. The solar panels in the roof cast odd prisms of light, particularly once the sun set. As it grew dark, the interior of the house itself seemed to dim into a stand-by glow, although brighter overheads would kick on via motion-detectors if you walked in the room.

It actually gave her the creeps – like the house was constantly watching you.

The skeleton of the giant prehistoric lizard in the middle of the lobby didn't help. Who could live like this?

"You don't ever get lonely?" Mona asked.

"I prefer solitude, Mrs. Watson," Burroughs said. "Some people are like that."

He eyed her knowingly. "I suspect you're not."

Mona shook her head politely. Her private belief was that most who claimed to prefer autonomy, did so out of the inability to fit in, not the desire.

Simple enough psychology – turn a failing into a virtue signal. As she looked around, she saw it on full display.

"We're happy to leave you to it," Colin said stiffly, "the moment we find our friend."

Mona glanced sideways at his tone – he clearly wasn't happy about staying the night. Despite what Burroughs had said, Mona could see Colin wanted to go out after Anna. She suspected the only reason he hadn't insisted, was because he wanted to be on hand when the rescue chopper arrived – which should not be long once the alarm was finally sent.

For her part, Mona was content to wait. It wasn't like she was going to be involved in any rescue. Her place would be at Anna's side when – *if* – they found her. At this point, Mona very much wanted 'official' channels to take over.

Not that she had any doubt in Colin's ability to scout the land in the dark, even among dragons. But the selfish truth was, after he'd left them on the beach, she'd been afraid. This time, she wanted him around.

She had half-considered suggesting they share a room tonight, but the look in Colin's eye told her he had other things on his mind.

Burroughs led them on a brief tour of the grounds.

"I want you to feel free to move about," he said, "but remember your safety depends on recognizing boundaries.

"This is the living area," he said. The staircase that had led them down from the roof was built around the central pillar, mirrored on the opposite side by wider, ballroom-style stairs that led up the half-level to the bedroom-floor, overlooking the lobby.

The panoramic view off the rear deck was like a movie screen.

Mounted on the wall, was a portrait of Lorena Burroughs.

Mona and Colin both exchanged glances.

"Your wife was very beautiful," Mona said, as Burroughs stepped up beside them.

In fact, Lorena Burroughs actually looked rather like Anna.

Although, Mona thought, a touch reproachful, Anna *was* that generically beautiful blond, and they all looked alike.

Mona had always been chagrined, working on her spin-machines like a fiend, while Anna, her figure carved from youth by dance-squad, hadn't attended an aerobics class since college. Oh, and *then* she puts on a pair of glasses because she's far-sighted, and all the guys say she looks 'smart'.

Burroughs had fallen silent, looking up at the picture, prominently displayed. Below the portrait was a small table, adorned with ordinary items, like a catch-shelf. Completely unremarkable. Except Mona could see why they were there.

Keys, a phone – clearly a woman's phone. A pair of fancy sunglasses. A shrine.

Five years, Mona thought. Where did that put you in the stages of grief? Considering how she had died?

Burroughs' professorial manner was a facade Mona had seen before – the lifelong academic. She actually found his authoritarian manner childlike, and felt rather sorry for him – the kid who had spent his lunch-hours alone in the library, now grown up and grown old.

The man looked up at the portrait of his wife as if he had lost her yesterday.

"I'm sorry," Mona said.

"Not at all," Burroughs said. "I like to talk about her." He nodded at the scattered items on the table. "I keep all her things. Her phone. All those silly little chirps and beeps and ringtones she used to like. She still gets them. All the telemarketing and auto-calls."

He smiled wistfully. "You asked me if I ever got lonely. The answer is, 'only if I think about it'."

Burroughs nodded, agreeing with a point he'd gone over in solitude many times.

"I have heard it said that love is biochemically no different than eating large quantities of chocolate. What that means is, if you provide the stimulus, only the mind knows the difference."

Burroughs tapped his head. "Therefore, you occupy the mind with other things. And the mind is easily distracted."

Mona shifted uncomfortably.

Colin listened with the expression of a man gaining reconnaissance.

"Psychology," Burroughs said, "is all about fulfilling needs. Simple things *work*. You will find you can program every mood with a scent, with a song, the taste of a snack. A little jingle on a cell-phone. Perhaps a gang of characters on a television show. In a world of virtual reality, there's no reason to be lonely. Or unhappy. Not ever.

"And if you really need to have someone's physical presence," he said, "you can simply order it online like a pizza."

Burroughs nodded to the portrait. "That was how *we* met."

He smiled at Mona's expression.

"It was nothing terribly complicated. I placed a singles-ad. 'Sugar-daddy seeks companion for remote tropical island.' Some such, like that." He shrugged. "I'm a practical man. I look to fulfill basic needs."

His face grew thoughtful.

"I think she understood that about me. It appealed to the realist in her. She answered the ad, after all, providing pictures."

Colin looked up at Lorena Burroughs – who so resembled Anna – and his face seemed to have cooled. Mona herself withheld judgment. She'd actually met Rodger in a similar manner.

"Still," Burroughs said, "human socio-biology works. Proximity, the act of consummation – over time, it builds a bond. As it does in many of the more advanced species. Fulfilling those physical needs. I loved her. After my fashion."

Now he led them out onto the back deck, overlooking the ocean.

The sun was setting, and that only made the view absolutely perfect.

"Wow," Mona said, pushing away from Colin's wing for the first time. "This is incredible."

Besides the Olympic-sized pool, there were hot tubs, a bar – five-star accommodations.

"This," Burroughs said, "was *my* part of the bargain."

For the first time, Mona could see the selling point. Assuming a credit-limit to go with it.

But then she glanced over the railing.

At its furthest point, the deck was a sheer drop, straight down to the ocean. But to either side, was the dragon pit.

Mona shuddered. This would have been where it happened.

She pushed away from the railing.

"Upstairs," Burroughs said, "was hers." He smiled at Mona. "I take it you approve?"

Mona nodded, politely, subdued.

"Downstairs," Burroughs said, "the basement, so to speak, was mine."

He chirped a bit of laughter. "Lorena didn't spend much time there. She definitely stuck to her part of the house."

"I'm afraid to ask," Mona said.
Now she saw the child in the professor again.
"Would you care to see?" he asked.

CHAPTER 19

The lower levels were like the engine room of a cruise-liner – the grimy mechanics under the ritzy illusion.

Colin had seen breeding facilities – croc farms, as well as reptile parks – but this was commercial scale. That it was being run by one person should have been overwhelming.

The automation Burroughs had mentioned was evident. The facility was broken into sections – eggs and incubation chambers, reminiscent of any chicken farm – as well as a surgical lab.

Then there were cages – young yearling dragons. With the concentration of adults on this island, if they were released at this size, they would be devoured.

The largest of these still-indoor animals was over four-feet, and separated from the others in its own little enclosure, like a holding cell before being released into the pit.

"We sometimes need to accommodate larger animals," Burroughs explained. "We've occasionally brought big ones back for medical attention and that sort of thing.

"More importantly, however," he said, turning their attention back to the stairway and the final level below, "this is the access-way to the rest of the island."

The garage level, Colin recalled, where the bridge crossed over the pit.

"Hypothetical," Burroughs said, pointing downstairs in the manner of a flight-attendant reciting safety-tips, "if the building's on fire, *this* is the direction you want to take."

He turned.

"*This* floor, however..."

Like the main lobby one level up, the lab-floor was split by an open patio, and deceptively solid glass/clear-alloy doors – which Burroughs unlocked and pushed open. The lights outside clicked on.

The deck stretched out over the pit.

Obviously, a feeding station. The circular deck mimicked the saucer-pattern of the Enterprise-dome above, and was built well away from the support struts that carried the weight of the building. The reason was clear – dragons were good climbers and the deck had to be inaccessible.

As the lights came on, the dragons below came scurrying.

Mona shrank into Colin's side. Colin dutifully lay his arm over her shoulder.

These lizards were the adolescents, even though they were the size of most full adults Colin had ever seen. And still not large enough to be safely released into the wild.

Sorry – the *preserve*.

The dragons stared up, expectantly, into the lights, gaping their mouths like baby vultures.

"Obviously," Colin said, "they know that someone coming out here means food."

The dragons hissed impatiently. Burroughs pressed a second button. Colin caught the scent of perfume wafting and the big lizards scattered.

Mona sniffed the air, confused. "Hot Kitty?"

Burroughs smiled. "Would you like to see something?"

He led them back to the enclosure where the transient three-footer sat sequestered.

As the dragon sat watching steadily, chest out like a lion, even at this more diminutive size, Burroughs opened the gate to the enclosure and stepped fully inside.

He extended his hand to the yearling dragon.

And just as the dragons had in the pit, the four-foot lizard came running...

... and placed its head into Burroughs' palm, just like a dog accepting a scratch on the neck.

Burroughs patted the creature, which clearly liked the attention.

Mona, whose nails had clenched into Colin's shoulder, now released hesitantly. "It's... like a dog."

Burroughs nodded. "They *are* quite intelligent."

Then he stepped back, producing a piece of chicken.

Now the dragon perched, waiting for the toss, snapping the raw meat out of the air – again, just like a dog.

It looked back up for more.

Burroughs tossed another piece of chicken.

At this point, Colin noted, there was no more petting. Not after it was feeding.

Because it really *wasn't* like a dog. Yes, it recognized you, and had been conditioned to respond to feeding and the pleasant scratch on the neck.

What it was missing was empathy – a return of affection. Accepting pleasurable attention from you didn't mean the lizard *liked* you the way the dog did.

Burroughs was activating very simple buttons. The moment the hand feeding resembled food, the lizard would very readily bite – and kill – *and* devour.

Lizards, particularly monitors, *were* smart, as reptiles go. But in no way did this intelligence manifest in anything like kindness. They hadn't evolved that far yet.

The trick to being around them was to never forget that.

Colin wondered if that might have been a contributing factor to what had happened to Burroughs' wife.

One thing you encountered a lot in the wild parts of the world was a preponderance of people who told generous versions of their past – invariably in ways that exonerated them from the circumstances that led them down such unsavory paths in the first place.

Colin had learned to sniff it. People told themselves the same stories for such a long time, they often came to nearly believing them. Colin wondered how much Burroughs might have tailored in his own mind, to suit a more favorable self-judgment.

For whatever reason, Colin's hackles were up.

Nothing, as far as he was concerned, was normal on this island.

The thought of Anna alone out there, caused his teeth to clench.

Check that, not alone – *captive.*

Of some nut even crazier than the guy they were depending on to get them all off this island.

And Colin very badly wanted off of this island.

Burroughs tossed a final piece of meat to the young dragon and it wolfed down the entire chunk.

Mona paled slightly as the thing's throat bulged like a snake's as it swallowed.

You never found dragon victims. They ate everything – feet with shoes still on.

Colin could guess what it had been like when Lorena Burroughs had fallen in among them – whose portrait looked so much like Anna.

He'd seen dragons in the wild. They would have come running, just like they did tonight. After a fifty-foot fall, you could only assume injury – if she even remained conscious, or even survived the fall at all, she doubtfully could have done nothing but lain there, broken and helpless, while the dragons jumped on her, biting and tearing.

No different than Colin had seen them do to a deer or a pig.

You couldn't train that part out of them. No matter what conditioning. That was another mistake you made when you started teaching them tricks like dogs.

"Ummm. Not to be impolite," Mona said, "but could we go back upstairs?"

Burroughs offered his thin smile. "It seems my demonstration has been lost on the lady. To be fair, my wife felt much the same way."

Burroughs performed a quick, dutiful clean-up, and shut off the lights.

The little monitor scurried to the back of the enclosure. Feeding time done.

"Shall we?" Burroughs said, turning abruptly for the stairs. "You must be hungry. And we still need to prep your rooms."

Mona followed quickly, anxious to leave these incubation under-bowels behind.

"First light," Colin said, raising his voice assertively up the stairs. "If you haven't raised an emergency line, I want to be out after them at first light."

Burroughs nodded placatingly over his shoulder, holding up his phone. "Agreed, Captain. Come along, please."

Colin paused, surveying the floor in the dim light of the terrariums, taking a mental snapshot – more reconnaissance, just in case.

He could see outside, where their movement had activated the floodlights out over the yard – and the fence right above the pit.

That big dragon was on the gate-post again, back on its perch.

It was staring in.

Colin wondered if it could see him.

"Captain?" Burroughs called from the stairway.

Colin turned. "Coming," he said, and begin to jog after them up the stairs.

Out on the fence, the dragon's eyes followed.

CHAPTER 20

Anna slept heavy. When she woke, it was full daylight and the sun was quickly growing warm. For a wonder, she actually felt better. Drained, but better.

At the cave entrance, the gate had been pulled away. Aching and sore, but at least rested, Anna peered outside cautiously.

The fire had burned low. There was no sign of Taylor.

Anna felt a momentary stab of fear. Had the dragons gotten him? Dragged him off?

No, she thought, her gate was open. That was Taylor. And if the dragons had gotten him after that, you'd think they'd have rooted her out too.

Or maybe that came later. Anna looked around nervously at the empty rocks.

What if he was really gone?

She saw Taylor's stick, leaning against the rocks. Would he have left *that* behind?

Anna snatched the stick up. She never played sports, but besides the dance team, she'd been a cheerleader, and also on the band – she could spin one mean baton.

When she heard the rocks clank behind her, she rose up ready, her heart pounding with refreshed adrenaline.

But it was Taylor edging down the stair-steps from the ridge above. He was carrying two buckets of water and what looked like a basket of eggs.

"I see we're feeling better," he said, as he opened the gate, stepping through and sealing it closed in deliberate ritual. He seemed utterly unconcerned as Anna brandished his own stick.

"I had to get water," he said. "I used up a lot of my supply keeping your fever down last night."

Anna held the stick in first position, just like she had when she'd twirled that big heavy flag back on the football field. It was a mistake to underestimate her.

"Oh," Taylor said, "thanks."

He set down both buckets and snatched the stick out of her grip as if she'd handed it to him.

"Here," he said, holding up the basket. "Breakfast."

Her empty hands still stinging, Anna looked doubtfully at the catch of eggs.

"Don't tell me those are..."

"Dragon eggs," Taylor nodded. "Best time to raid the nests is mid-morning. That's when they try and catch those morning rays, before the sun gets too hot."

He picked up one of the brownish, leathery shells. "I try to eat as many of them as I can. Gives them something to think about."

"They don't really think like that, do they?"

"No. But if nests keep getting despoiled, they'll move. It's just instinct." He tossed the egg back in the bucket.

"Besides," he said, "it's symbolic. At this point, it's personal to *me*. I want something that'll *hurt*."

"So, just a random act of cruelty? For no greater reason than that?"

Taylor considered. "Well. There's '*fuck* them' and *that's* why."

He cast her an arched eye as he poured water into a cooking pot, along with the bucket of eggs, propping it up over the fire.

"You know, you'd think I'd deserve an outlet."

It was bizarre, Anna thought. Even as she pressed back against the rock wall, he fussed about the clearing, as if this was an argument they'd been having for years.

Yeah, she thought. NOT quite stable.

What was worse, she actually felt herself falling into the part. The power of projection.

Now he seemed to be 'making-up'.

"Look," he said, his tone conciliatory, "I have to get more water. We're still low. Will you be alright alone?"

Anna blinked. What was the correct response here?

She simply stayed silent. Taylor pursed his lips.

"Okay, fine, be like that."

He grabbed up two more buckets, but before he left, he handed her one of the squirt bottles of bleach.

"Here. Hold onto this until I get back. Aim for the eyes." He looked at her meaningfully. "Do *not* try to use it on me."

He tipped his wrist at an imaginary watch. "I'll be about twenty minutes."

In a bit of a huff, he pushed open the gate, always taking care to secure it back again. He took the stair-steps up to the ridge at an irritated lope.

Anna looked at the squirt-bottle in her hands. Her earlier confidence had utterly evaporated, but the little plastic nozzle was rather therapeutic – it actually felt comfortingly like a small pistol.

She set it to straight-stream.

Taylor said aim for the eyes. He wanted something that would hurt.

Anna was not entirely unsympathetic. Crazy was how you got. But that didn't change the fact that *she* had to deal with it.

She had to find the others.

They were barely a couple of miles away. She knew the direction. And Taylor had just told her the dragons were out sunning themselves.

And she had her bottle of bleach.

Setting her teeth, she began to pull at the rocks bracing the barricade, and was surprised to find they wouldn't even budge. Taylor had rolled them aside with one arm and a grunt.

Crazy strength, Anna thought. Or Neanderthal.

She began climbing gingerly over the top. Fortunately, most of the sharpened stakes and tangles of vine were oriented to keep dragons *out*, not to keep a person in. Anna actually perched on the broadest stake as she hopped off the top onto the rocky ledge.

Following the stair-step path to the ridge, she peered cautiously up over the top, scanning the volcanic tundra beyond.

Taylor was nowhere to be seen. He had gone after water – presumably a stream – which meant one of the falls Anna had seen draining water on either side of the beach.

Therefore, *she* was headed straight through the trees. Two and a half miles northeast – a distance she could jog in twenty minutes.

The morning, however, was already growing uncomfortably hot, even under the canopy. In stark contrast to the salty dry coast, Anna could feel the heavy moisture like a humid soup – not to mention her bikini hadn't exactly been cut with the idea of hiking rough-shewn country – she was quickly tiger-striped from slashing leaves and branches.

She kept as much as she could under the trees, with less ground foliage and easier on her bare legs – and fewer places to hide for anything that might try and bite.

Two-and-a-half miles. Twenty minutes.

Within sixty-seconds, she was forced to stop, gasping, her body loudly reminding her she was only *better,* not *well* – and probably could stand a hospital stay. Running cross-country wasn't helping. The sixteen-ounce plastic bottle of bleach, held in a pistol-grip, felt like a ten-pound weight. She caught a whiff of her own cave-sweat and BO.

She wondered if the dragons could smell it too. Anna eyed the long grass mistrustfully. She squirted a little bit of bleach in the air behind her.

Deterrent.

Although not a fail-safe.

Trying to control her breathing, and moving smoothly, so as not to cramp her over-taxed muscles, Anna began to jog. If the dragons were on the move again, twenty-minutes might make a difference.

That's assuming she was going the right way. She was dead-lining the direction Taylor kept pointing over his shoulder.

Of course, he *was* crazy.

Five more minutes and Anna was again forced to rest

But now she realized that the trees were thinning up ahead. She had reached the opposite coast.

Almost there. Urgently – and perhaps a bit impatiently – she took her first step before fully catching her wind, again underestimating how physically depleted she had really been. She stumbled, falling forward, landing hard, chopping skin from her bare legs.

Anna squeezed tears. Sucking breath, she rose painfully to her knees.

Rising with her, no more than a foot from her nose, was a cobra, hood spread.

The tongue flicked, just like the dragon's.

Anna's breath let loose in a slow, paralyzed rasp.

She didn't know much about cobras – or even if it really *was* a cobra – there were lots of elapid relatives that spread hoods – and they were all very venomous.

Or it could be a spitter that would spray her eyes and leave her blind and writhing on the forest floor.

Anna hung motionless, as the cobra hovered, its mouth slightly agape. The creature's head was no larger than her two fingers together. She could see the tiny fangs – a scratch was all it needed.

And then, abruptly, the cobra dropped its hood. Suddenly no more remarkable than an ordinary garter snake, it slithered off into the bushes.

Anna inhaled slowly.

"*Ohhhhh*," she exhaled, "FUCK this place!"

She clambered to her feet. She had dropped her bleach-bottle as she fell, and now saw it split open and empty on the rocks.

Not even a bottle of bleach.

She chirped a snort of laughter.

As if.

She touched at the blood running down her legs and bent to inspect the cuts – but movement behind her caught her eye.

A flicking tail above the grass.

Over the camouflaging blades, a snake-like head popped up.

The eyes blinked, then turned and found her.

If it had been standing next to her, Anna estimated it would have reared up above her waist.

She also realized why the snake had retreated. Dragons *ate* cobras. Taylor told her that. In fact, Anna had seen it herself on the Discovery Channel – monitors gobbling snakes right up, immune to venom, utterly ignoring inconsequential bites on their leathered hides.

She looked down at the fresh blood splattering her leg.

The dragon's lolling tongue tasted the scent on the breeze.

Anna turned and began to run.

The coast was just ahead. She was almost home.

But she also felt the toxic burn of lactic acid threatening to cramp her up, and knew a knotted-muscle would drop her in her tracks.

She took a breath, settling back into slower, deliberate moves, stretching her muscles the way she had learned in dance, when you cramped during a routine, keeping her limbs moving at right-angles, stretching the muscles like rubber-bands.

It probably looked ridiculous, fleeing through the jungle, skipping along like a ballet dancer.

The path was finally too rocky for cover, and the dragon emerged from the tall grass. After a moment, a second lizard joined it.

Both dragons scented the air, tongues snaking in and out.

As if out for a morning walk, the two of them began strolling her way.

Somehow, that deliberate, unhurried pace made it worse – like a slasher-flick-stalker – the unkillable masked-psycho who just WALKED after you – but still seemed to stay right on your tail, no matter how hard you ran. Implacable and silent.

Anna would run until she was exhausted and they would just follow. They tasted your trail, that lolling tongue leading those teeth inexorably ever-closer.

They were cold-blooded – you'd think they'd get tired.

Except, why would they? They just walked. Hell, they stayed in the shade.

But the pursuit was relentless. They had probably been tracking her for some time. There was also very likely, more of them.

Up ahead, the foliage finally broke apart, and Anna stepped out of the forest cover onto the east shore of the island.

A quick appraisal of the sun and the angle of the coast suggested she was still probably a little bit south of where she needed to be.

But as she looked up the coastline, she now saw what looked bizarrely like a medieval castle silhouetted by the mid-morning sun.

"You've got to be kidding," Anna said aloud.

Behind her, a third dragon emerged from the tall grass.

Anna began to run.

CHAPTER 22

Colin had been serious about the light of day, and was ready to make an issue over it, but when Colin appeared downstairs, Burroughs was already up on his morning rounds. He met Colin at the stairs, carrying a cup of coffee.

He also had two bolt-action 30.06s and handed one to Colin.

"Aim for the head," Burroughs said. "And don't expect the others to stop once you start shooting."

He eyed Colin seriously. "It's best not to *have* to."

Marcus was still out, sleeping deep with painkillers, but Colin had roused Mona, knocking on her door.

The door had opened a crack, and a bleary eye peered out.

"We're going out to find her," Colin said.

Mona pulled the door open.

"There's still no contact? There's still no one coming for us?"

Colin nodded to Burroughs who shrugged, shaking his head.

"We'll find her," Colin said. "You check in on Marcus."

Mona nodded, frightened all over again.

Truth to tell, Colin wasn't sure what to make of it. Yes, contact broke up in this part of the world – all the time. He also understood the psychological proclivity, when something happens just so perfectly *wrong*, to attribute deliberate intent.

Colin took a moment to evaluate his own faculties. There was no deliberate intent in the wave that had sent them adrift for two days – or that big shark that had taken Rodger Vaughn.

It was frustrating to recognize your own weakness, but Colin knew he was as susceptible to trauma and physical exhaustion as anyone. He might not be operating on his best judgment right now – which was why he was still ceding to Burroughs.

Even though something felt wrong.

It felt that way when Burroughs led him down to the garage, waiting for the chugging door to slowly open, only to have the Jeep itself die right there in front of the bridge.

Colin felt his temper tick by degrees as Burroughs puttered on repairs. First light was already becoming mid-morning.

In his steady, meticulous way, Burroughs traded spark plugs, removed the battery and hooked it to a charger – very efficiently – Colin couldn't have done it any faster.

It was just the perfect *wrongness* of it that set his teeth grinding.

Next, they were going to find the damn bridge-gate was stuck.

Colin found himself irritated at Burroughs' ambling manner –
efficiency or no efficiency, he wanted to see a little damned *urgency*.

That was where he reminded himself he was strung-out.

Burroughs tightened the last bolt, and was about to test the ignition,
when there was a sudden clanging alarm.

"Security," Burroughs said, "is set to detect motion over four-feet
high."

"Detecting people instead of dragons," Colin said, understanding.

"We may have a stroke of luck, Captain Braddock."

Burroughs tapped the nearest console and brought up the security
cameras.

"Is this your lady friend, Captain?"

The motion-detectors had been activated along the same path Colin
had followed, and he realized now he had been on camera all along.

The figure on-screen was a stumbling scarecrow in a bikini. She was
trying to run, but barely managed a lurching half-trot.

Colin remembered the shape Anna had been in on the beach, and
knew he was seeing a heroic last-ditch effort to survive.

"That's her," Colin said.

"She's still about half-a-mile up the road," Burroughs said. "And
look here."

He turned the video manually to the background behind her.

Colin counted at least three dragons, strolling between twenty and
thirty yards behind her, just as casual as you please.

No urgency.

Colin grabbed up his rifle. "Let's go," he said.

Burroughs turned the key in the ignition and the Jeep roared to life,
rolling out onto the bridge...

… where they waited as the gate opened... *slowly.*

Colin twisted in his seat. A half-mile up the road. A couple of
minutes?

But even as he thought it, the gate hitched on its gears and ground to
a stop – perfectly wrong.

Then the gate kicked again and rolled the rest of the way open.
Burroughs wasted no time beyond the bridge with perfume, scattering any
dragons that lurked outside the gate with tear-gas.

And perhaps finally sensing urgency, Burroughs spun tires, skidding
the Jeep out onto the dirt road.

Colin gripped his rifle.

Half a mile.

CHAPTER 23

Anna didn't know she'd set off alarms. She didn't know help was on its way. Nor could she see how close she was. All she knew was that she was hurt, bleeding, and there were three dragons on her tail, pacing her until that moment she finally stumbled.

The greatest tragedies were those who gave up, never knowing how close they were to success.

Well, Anna wasn't going to quit. The sheer horror of being torn apart and devoured by these *things* precluded that.

But she *would* eventually stumble and fall.

With salvation – such as it may be – somewhere, only just ahead.

Still out of sight. She had no idea how far.

The point, however, became moot when she did indeed trip again, landing heavily and hard.

Behind her, all three dragons bolted forward as one.

Stunned, Anna struggled to her knees.

But the dragons were in range now – cashing in that judicial expense of energy to deliver a debilitating bite to the weakening prey.

The first of them closed, snapping for her calf.

And then, somehow, as if he'd been lurking in the surrounding brush all along, Taylor was there.

The pronged stick was out, catching the snapping dragon's head, even as the teeth turned angrily back at him. The big-lizard thrashed wildly, lashing its bony-tail like a bullwhip.

Anna saw Taylor flinch as the tip slashed his face.

"Bastard!" he cursed, and now he pulled a bleach-bottle sidearm, launching a stream at the lizard's eyes.

There was a steam-vent hiss as the dragon twisted in agony, bolting for the bushes.

The other two dragons paused, catching the foul scent. With his stick up, Taylor advanced until he was in range, and began firing the squirt-bottle like a pistol, adding a couple of quick prompts with the end of his stick. He kept after them until they retreated.

Anna looked up from the ground as he turned, eyeing her darkly.

"I am *so* sorry," she said, holding up her bleeding hands placatingly.

Shaking his head, Taylor had started to move towards her when a gunshot rang out.

Anna saw a spurt of blood as Taylor was knocked over backwards, landing with a heavy grunt.

Now she heard the sound of a car door slam, and Colin's voice, "What the hell are you *doing?*"

A large Jeep pickup had appeared on the road ahead of them, and Anna saw Colin jump from the passenger side.

Leaning out the driver's side was an older man. He was holding a smoking rifle over the open door.

Doctor Burroughs, Anna presumed.

Who, Taylor said, had been trying to kill him for five years.

And now, he might just have done it.

Clambering to his knees, holding his gut, Taylor looked up as Burroughs again took aim.

Colin, however, caught the barrel and pushed it down, even as Taylor gained his feet and started to run.

"Damn it!" Burroughs cursed, pushing Colin's hands away, raising his rifle again.

But Taylor had already vanished, disappearing into the thick brush as quickly as the dragons.

"I got you *that* time," Burroughs said, as he scanned the surrounding foliage. "You slippery son of a bitch."

"Forget him!" Colin said angrily, bending over Anna. "Let's get her inside!"

Burroughs eyed the bushes a moment longer, before turning to look at Anna full in the face for the first time.

The old-gentleman's eyes widened and he momentarily froze in his tracks – much as Taylor had, himself.

Burroughs took a hesitant step forward, like a dog sniffing at a once-familiar person who had been gone for a long time.

"That scent," he said, "Hot Kitty?"

Anna blinked up at him. "*He* sprayed me with it. He said it was a deterrent."

Burroughs nodded. "Yes. I'll bet he would."

Now he blinked, self-aware.

"I'm sorry. It's just that... you remind me of someone."

Anna shifted uncomfortably. "That's what *he* said."

"Yes," Burroughs said again. "I'll bet he did."

He spared one final glare at the brush where Taylor had disappeared, before turning to help Colin with Anna.

"Come on," he said. "Let's get you back to the house."

CHAPTER 24

Colin carried Anna upstairs from the garage at a full jog. Burroughs puffed, trying to keep up.

"Boy," Colin said, as Anna clung to him like Tarzan swinging through the trees, "he wasn't kidding with that Hot Kitty, was he? Were you on a date?"

Anna summoned the strength to slap him across the chest, even as Colin hip-bumped the door to the infirmary. Both Marcus and Mona sat up, wide-eyed.

"Anna!" Marcus cried.

"Oh, *honey*," Mona fluttered, immediately beside her, cradled in Colin's arms.

Stepping in behind them, somewhat out of breath, Burroughs promptly grabbed up his lab smock, per-ritual, and began prepping the med-unit.

"Well, Mr. Miller," he said, turning to Marcus. "I think you're as stitched up as you need to be. Care to give up the bed for the lady?"

Grunting painfully, Marcus hopped off the mattress onto his one good foot, catching his balance as Burroughs performed a prompt and efficient linen-change – sixty-seconds or less – allowing Colin to lay Anna down on the clean sheets.

Mona took Marcus' shoulder, steadying him on his good foot as he bent by Anna's side.

"I thought I lost you."

Anna allowed the attention. But Colin saw her eyes flick uncomfortably in his own direction.

And when Marcus tried to kiss her lips, he got her cheek. There was a heartbeat of uncomfortable silence as every person in the room pretended not to notice.

Marcus made a show of squeezing her hand.

Burroughs finally broke the awkward silence.

"I'll give you a moment together," he said, nodding to Colin. "Captain, if you would give me a hand, while I set up a room for Mr. Miller?"

Burroughs turned reassuringly to Anna. "You're going to need some fluids, maybe a few stitches. But you're going to be alright."

Colin followed Burroughs outside. The old man made a point of closing the infirmary door behind them, saying nothing as he led them to a hallway closet, from which he produced a collapsible wheelchair. Burroughs snapped the lightweight construct together, presenting it to Colin.

"Here," he said, "give this to Mr. Miller while I make up \

Colin reached for the chair, but Burroughs held it steady, e

directly.

"You've got designs on her, don't you?"

Colin frowned. "What are you talking about?"

"I can see it in your eyes," Burroughs said. "And there is a look in her eyes as well."

Colin took an impatient breath. "How is that any of your business?"

Burroughs was utterly unaffected by the younger man's scowl.

"An affair?"

Colin sighed, glancing back towards the infirmary.

"No," he said, keeping his voice low. "It... was a long time ago."

Strangely enough, Colin found he actually felt compelled to speak. The old guy had a bit of Perry Mason in him.

Or perhaps, just once, he simply wanted to say it out loud.

"If we'd met five minutes earlier," Colin said, "it might have all been different. But her friend hit on me first. That would be Mona, by the way – which threw Anna into the wing-man spot. And that was how she met Marcus. No deeper than that."

Colin shook his head in ten-year old frustration.

"Honest to God, I didn't even *like* Marcus that much. He was just this annoying little guy who hung around after I chased off a couple of bullies one night. It didn't mean we were life-long buddies. I needed a roommate for six months, and he paid his share of the rent.

"But because of that, he got handed the girl of my dreams. And yes, I think it's goddamn unfair."

"Yet," Burroughs said, "she is now another man's wife."

Colin glanced back to the infirmary, visible through the window, with Marcus still bent over one side, holding Anna's hand, while she seemed to be paying most of her attention to Mona.

"Perhaps not for long," Colin said.

"You know," Burroughs said, "there was a man who was similarly infatuated with my wife. I remember how *I* felt about that man. Do you really want someone feeling that way about *you*?"

Point taken, Colin thought. That man in question was currently running around the bushes with a rifle-shot in his gut.

Of course, in the same situation, Marcus would have missed.

"He's hardly a threat," Colin said.

And with that, he turned, pushing the wheelchair back to the infirmary.

"You should take caution," Burroughs called after him, "when dealing with such a basic primal instinct."

Colin turned and looked back.

"As should we all," he said.

CHAPTER 25

Anna didn't yet know what to make of Richard Burroughs. He was clearly waiting to clear the room, allowing a bare minimum of due attention before ushering everyone off with assigned duties.

He settled a protesting Marcus into his wheelchair, handing him off to Colin.

"I can walk," Marcus said, but Burroughs held him fast.

"You *can*, but you shouldn't. Please Mr. Miller. Just be patient and let yourself get better. So I can attend to your wife."

Colin grabbed the handles on the chair, patting Marcus on the shoulder. "I'll see that he stays sitting."

Marcus acquiesced, dolefully.

Burroughs turned to Mona. "And it couldn't hurt to have some help getting dinner started."

That almost made Anna laugh. Mona left cooking to well-paid servants.

"Don't look at *me*," Mona said.

Colin sighed, pushing Marcus in his wheelchair over to Mona, and handing her the room key. "*I'll* get the kitchen going."

He turned before he left, tipping a concerned nod to Anna, with absolutely appropriate eye-contact.

"You're going to be okay," he said.

"Thank you, Colin," Anna responded, absolutely appropriately. But then, because she couldn't help herself, added, "... for everything."

Not quite so appropriately.

Colin paused at the door, glancing briefly at Marcus before stepping off quickly down the hall.

Mona cast a knowing look at Anna over Marcus' shoulder, as she began to push his chair. Marcus caught the door with one hand, looking back at his wife.

"I love you, Anna," he said.

Anna paused, honestly considering her answer – a moment of excruciating silence.

"I love you too," she said finally.

And it was true – but she got the tone just right. She knew because instead of smiling, Marcus cut his eyes away, deflated, as Mona bumped his chair out into the hall. Mona, who had referred to Marcus as a 'wishy-washy pussy', actually looked down at him with a degree of pity, as she nodded Anna goodnight.

I love you, could mean anything you wanted it too.

In this case, it meant, *I'm sorry.*

He simply wasn't what she wanted, and to keep going on was living a lie.

She was sorry, because she knew he doted on her – and she *did* feel genuine affection. He was a good guy.

But he was no Tarzan.

Anna shut her eyes, recalling how Colin had ran with her up the stairs, cradling her, effortlessly. She had tucked her head into his shoulder, like a baby duck. The comfort was like a warm fire in the cold, and when he had laid her out in the clean sheets, she had clung to him.

Now that he was gone again, she already felt that safe glow of comfort evaporate like heat from a teacup.

It didn't help being left alone with Burroughs.

The old man made no large movements as he busied about the infirmary. He was the sort Anna could not picture running or jumping, but who might walk fifty miles in a day.

He turned, holding a needle and thread, and brandishing a hypodermic – although she was at least gratified to see *this* needle didn't look like a stabbing weapon. She rubbed one hand over her still-tender glutes.

"I must remind you," Burroughs said, apparently determined to erode any remaining confidence, "I am not a medical doctor."

"So why am I letting you touch me?"

Burroughs smiled. "Lack of options."

Anna stared back, mistrustfully. His disarming smile didn't touch his eyes.

"I have, however," Burroughs continued, "a great deal of practice, in the area of sutures and general first-aid. If I may say so, I did a fine job on your husband's leg. He should heal completely, with minimal scarring."

Burroughs set the hypodermic aside, simply running his fingers the length of her arms, taking stock of her abrasions and cuts.

"As near as I can tell," he said, "you' haven't even been bitten. You do have a couple of bad lacerations, though."

He shook his head as if frankly surprised.

"All told, you are very lucky. All of you are."

Anna looked at him, trying to reconcile the image of the small, foppish, rather mild-looking man versus the fevered first-impression provided her by Taylor.

Burroughs' manner actually left her a bit cautious – which was perhaps not so surprising. Intense beliefs were the most contagious, especially in close quarters. It was the age-old question – lock-up a lunatic with a psychiatrist for twenty years, do you get two psychiatrists, or two lunatics?

Well, Anna thought ruefully, she was no psychiatrist, but in less than twenty-four hours, she had picked up Taylor's paranoia.

Of course, it wasn't paranoia if they were really out to get you. And not an hour ago, Burroughs had shot a bullet through him.

Anna let this stranger explore her body, cataloging her tally of injuries. To his credit, his hands were deft, and he was careful not to hurt her, even while dabbing bits of disinfectant.

He held up his needle. "With your permission, I'm going to give you a light sedative. Give you a chance to rest."

He asked politely, as opposed to flipping her over and poking her butt-cheek like a pincushion. Burroughs' hands were quick and deft as he administered the shot with barely a sting.

Almost immediately, Anna felt her muscles melt as the relaxant circulated directly into her blood. For the first time in days, the full-body ache faded, and she nearly groaned with relief.

She looked up at Burroughs, who was speaking again, and he sounded like he was underwater – something about checking on her later – bringing dinner.

For a moment, she let herself drift.

The next thing she was aware of was Burroughs setting a dinner tray by her bed. The shadows had grown long.

She sat up suddenly, starting awake, and was immediately greeted by fresh soreness.

"Ah. You're awake," Burroughs said. He leaned over, checking her eyes, and then her pulse.

"Alright, Mrs. Miller, you have two fairly bad gashes, assorted other minor cuts and bruises. Nothing quite requiring stitches."

Burroughs smiled, making an effort. "I'm happy to say, you're going to be just fine."

Then, for a long moment, he just looked at her.

Anna shifted uncomfortably. Realizing it, Burroughs sat back quickly, turning his attention to cleaning her dressings.

"I apologize," he said, embarrassed, "I don't mean to stare. But my wife – you *do* look remarkably like her."

Again there was that strange incongruence in his eyes, as if what was going on in his head had nothing to do with his face.

"I'm sorry," he said, "it just makes me miss her for a moment."

"She's been gone five years?" Anna asked.

Burroughs paused, looking up from the bandage on her leg.

"Yes." He eyed her closely. "Mr. Taylor told you that? He talked about her?"

Anna resisted the urge to swallow.

"He... uh... no. Just like I told you. I reminded him of... your wife."

Burroughs nodded seriously.

"I daresay, Mrs. Miller, that is what saved your life. You were lucky to survive his company."

Lucky to survive, *period*, Anna thought, but stayed silent.

"You never know about people," Burroughs said. He finished taping Anna's knee, his hands tracing the injury gently. Anna could see how he could have been a medical doctor. That was a hand that could work a scalpel.

"In a way, I suppose we were rather similar," he said. "We both shared a touch of an obsessive personality, and a tendency to fixate on subjects of great interest. Most often, a positive quality. It creates drive, promotes success. Great interest is necessary for professional-level expertise in any trade. Most people channel it into mundane pursuits. Some become doctors, some lawyers. Or even musicians or artists.

"And some of us," he said, "develop odd interests. Venomous snakes. Crocodilians. Sharks. Komodo dragons. Mr. Taylor and I shared a common interest."

Burroughs sighed. "As it turned out, more than one."

"Your wife?" Anna said – rather ham-handedly, her tongue loosened by the Demerol.

Burroughs gently dotted gauze over her shin. Then he pulled a rip of tape.

"Lorena," he said. "Yes."

"I'm sorry," Anna said, doubtfully. "I didn't mean..."

Burroughs interrupted, waving her off.

"Mrs. Miller, please. It's quite alright."

He attached the tape, and sat back, regarding her frankly.

"My wife wasn't happy. And the most luxurious accommodations couldn't change that. Her needs were more complex. Apparently, money and luxury lose their luster with isolation. Even Twitter is spotty out here."

"Couldn't she travel?"

"Oh, sure," Burroughs said. "But part of the deal was that she *lived* here. Not traveling the world on my money."

Anna nodded. That was how Mona would have done it.

"I realize how cold-blooded it sounds. Lorena always said I was a little too... reptilian."

Burroughs frowned thoughtfully. "I've wondered since what she meant when she said that. At the time, I thought she was calling me emotionless.

"But she was very perceptive, my wife," he said. "Reptiles are not emotionless. They are, in fact, *pure* emotion, and react purely and absolutely. It's called 'instinct'.

"The difference," he said, "with reptiles, is that there are only a few emotions of which they are capable."

Burroughs extended his own hands, exhibiting scars from many bites

91

over the years.

"I have had snakes, crocodiles and lizards of all kinds as pets, and I can attest that empathy is not a reptilian trait.

"So," he said, "perhaps that was what she meant. That I was not capable of higher-emotion. That my... passions.... were very basic."

Anna wished someone would come in the room. Burroughs' personal tone, the presumed familiarity – it was uncomfortably like how Taylor had acted.

Okay, she decided, they were *both* nuts.

"But the thing about empathy," Burroughs said, "it doesn't exist without an 'other'. In the absence of human comfort, I imagine we all can become quite reptilian."

The thin smile brushed his lips again.

"Ironic that I was counting on a little basic, mammalian, human contact-bonding. Simple behavioral sociology. You put the ingredients together, they rise like bread."

Burroughs smiled sadly.

"And it worked out just like that. Although, apparently, only for me."

Anna had heard one version of this story, but there was clearly more she didn't want to know. Her better instincts urged her to stay silent, and maybe she wouldn't have to hear it.

She asked anyway.

"What happened to your wife, Mr. Burroughs?"

Burroughs' old-world poise seemed to flicker, revealing a shadow of something dark and grim below.

"The dragons," he said, "tore her apart."

CHAPTER 26

"You know," Burroughs said, "I was four years old the first time I saw Komodo dragons kill someone."

The old man let the remark hang. After a moment, he stood and began shutting down the infirmary, returning each container, dropping utensils immediately into solution.

Anna stayed silent. She wasn't sure if the droop of Demerol made it better or worse.

"It's one thing to watch a person die," Burroughs said. "It's quite another when it's a *bad* death. The harsh truths of mortality and what can happen to a physical body are universal lessons."

He puttered through his clean-up – the rocking monkey.

"My father," he said, "was a very respected herpetologist, who naturally took his son with him on his jaunts around the world. From a very young age, I learned to be around reptiles. I learned to feed them, care for them. Most importantly, I learned what was safe behavior around them.

"My father was very stern," Burroughs said. "It didn't matter whether he was feeding a python or a monitor, when he gave them their dinner, he made sure I saw what they *did* to that live rabbit. And then he said, 'If you fell in there, that would be *you*'."

Brutal, Anna thought, but reasonable enough, all things considered. Her own mother had taken her out to the street when she was little to look at a gory, smashed cat, and told her, "*That's* why I don't want you playing in the road!"

She wondered what her mother might have showed her if she'd grown up on a crocodile-farm.

Burroughs closed the last cabinet and shut the lights off over the sink, leaving Anna sitting under the one light above her bed. Burroughs sat down beside her.

Anna braced herself. For whatever reason, he had decided to tell his story.

Second-hand absolution? She looked so much like his wife, after all.

"My parents," Burroughs said, "often traveled with another family. They had a young son, who was slightly older. We were like cousins who saw each other on vacation. South America on several occasions, or various parts of Africa, literally cruising on the Nile.

"This particular trip," he said, "was to the dragon islands."

Anna shut her eyes, and was punished with instant vertigo. Without even knowing any details, her semi-drugged dream-state already conjured any number of graphic, gory possibilities.

"We never even made it onto the island," Burroughs said. "Really, it was the only way what happened, *could* have happened. On the tour itself, everyone would have been more on their guard.

"The entrance," he said, "crosses a bridge, which you access from a boat, and you check-in at the Ranger's gate. Quite often, there are dragons lounging under the structure, especially in the early morning, and there was on this day. My father was an old-time colleague of the head ranger and we paused on the bridge for a brief reunion. My young friend and I were looking through the railing at the dragons below. I remember holding my mother's hand."

Burroughs shrugged. "No one really knew what actually happened. There were no cameras in those days. The ruling was that he must have slipped."

"You didn't see it?"

"I didn't remember," Burroughs said. "My parents said I was white as ghost, and that I didn't speak for several days." He shook his head. "I was four years old. At the time, all I remembered was that he was there, and then he was gone.

"And then, seeing the dragons pulling at something on the other side of the railing, and my parents pulling me away."

Burroughs held up his hands. "There," he said. "Not exactly war trauma. But maybe good for a complex or two."

Fair enough, Anna thought.

"Certainly," he said, "enough to have difficulty dealing with how Lorena died."

"I can imagine," Anna said.

Burroughs' eyes sharpened.

"He talked about what happened to her?"

Anna blinked at the sudden scrutiny. "Well... he said she died. He mentioned the dragons. He said the deterrents... didn't work." She shook her head apologetically. "We were only together one night."

Burroughs studied her face.

`There were certain tells when a person lied, usually little ticks of expression, the pulling back of eyes – the *fear* expression. Anna had seen it demonstrated in slow-motion videos of people known to be lying. It was a basic involuntary reaction.

Tonight, however, Anna was heavily stoned – the muscles in her face were slack.

"I think... maybe he blames himself," she said.

The deflection worked. Burroughs' eyes darkened.

"I know *I* do," he said. "He put his *hands* on her..."

Anna remembered those hands.

"She was fighting," Burroughs said. "I tried to intercede..."

He shut his eyes, as if helpless not to see it.

"She went over the edge. The dragons took her in seconds. And trust me, *this* time I remembered every bit of it.

"Taylor," he said, "escaped into the jungle. He went over the ledge, and then jumped the fence."

Anna frowned. "He jumped fifty-feet? Is he crazy? Why didn't the dragons attack him?"

"They were occupied," Burroughs said. "With her."

"And yes," he said, "he's quite crazy. I didn't see how he got down. By the time I looked over, he was already jumping the perimeter fence. That was the last I ever saw of him. Until today."

Burroughs considered the implications.

"It's remarkable. This is such a small island. I *tried* to find him and gave up. I assumed the dragons had gotten him. They don't leave much behind. Clothes, shoes. They digest it all."

Burroughs shook his head. "But all this time, he was out there. It almost gives me the creeps. I imagine he's quite mad by now."

He looked at Anna. "You met him. What was *your* impression?"

Anna's impression was pretty much that.

"Why haven't you called the authorities?"

"Jurisdiction is indefinite out here. Quite frankly, I thought he was dead."

Then his eyes hardened. "And maybe," he said, "because it was nobody else's business."

Abruptly, he stood.

"As for Mr. Taylor, if that shot doesn't kill him, he's out there bleeding, and this time the dragons will track him down. I can't say that I care which. Sometimes the old rules are best."

Besides, Anna thought, you want something that'll *hurt*.

She wondered what Burroughs would say if he knew the things Taylor had told her. She actually had to resist the urge – something about the old-gentleman's penetrating manner activated a confessional-response. He presented as *authority*.

But there was no possible good outcome to throwing anything Taylor had to say on the record. At best, she would be insulting the man who saved all their lives, offered medical attention and shelter, and in who their immediate future still depended upon.

And gosh, if there weren't a lot of other reasons to keep quiet, if even a smidgen of what Taylor told her was true.

Anna was not sure yet *who* she believed – if either – or both.

The real truth, Anna had found, was almost never in the middle.

Burroughs was still staring at her from the door.

"You really *do* look like Lorena," he said. "And Taylor said so too? *And* he followed you back onto the grounds?"

Burroughs hung his head regretfully.

"The possibility occurs to me that he might now have fixated on *you*."

A possibility that Anna actually had not considered.

"Get some rest, Mrs. Miller," Burroughs said. "I'll check on you later."

He closed the door behind him, shutting off the main light, leaving only the small lamp over Anna's bed.

Anna tried to shut her eyes. Despite her exhaustion, despite the Demerol, she felt like she'd chewed a caffeine tablet.

Because she believed Taylor *was* in fact out there. She very much doubted the dragons had caught him.

And yes, on short acquaintance, he did seem to trend a bit obsessive.

He had followed her back. Just like Kong followed Fay Wray.

That meant he was likely somewhere close.

Anna shut off her light, and lay in the dark, sleepless, with open eyes.

Listening for things that went bump in the night.

CHAPTER 27

Marcus was in a lot of pain. The drugs Burroughs had given him earlier allowed him to sit at the table for dinner, propped up in his wheelchair, but now they were wearing off. In the ensuing hours the only time he forgot about his throbbing leg was because he touched the tentacle-burn on his face.

Burroughs had applied ointment to the burn, but had been non-committal about the scarring potential – meaning he might now simply have what looked like a sword slash across the middle of his face. Disfigured was the word.

Dinner, at least, had been a mostly festive occasion. Anna was safe. For Marcus, not much else mattered, so long as they would be getting off this island soon.

Burroughs, however, had taken the occasion to announce that communications were still down.

"But," he said, "tomorrow, I will fire up one of my short-wave radios, and call for help. They require minor repair, which has not been a priority until everyone was safe. But I promise you, one way or another, we will be raising someone within twenty-four hours."

Colin frowned but said nothing. Mona had refilled her wine glass.

Marcus, however, for the first time, allowed himself to wonder what happened after. By tomorrow at this time, they would be back in the world. Factor another seventy-two hours for hospital visits and official red-tape, and then they would be put back into their lives.

At which point, some long-standing decisions would have to be made.

For himself, one of those decisions was made as Colin wheeled him back to his room after dinner.

"I'm going to fight for her," Marcus said.

Colin stiffened slightly.

Marcus watched his friend's face – a friendship based on six-months, ten years ago.

Colin had been very careful about appearances, betraying absolutely nothing inappropriate. But Marcus was no fool. And one thing he'd learned was that people show the most by what they hide, like a shadow puppet on the wall.

"I beg your pardon?" Colin said, preserving the fiction.

Marcus recognized it. Fine, he'd preserve it too.

"Anna and I have been having problems," he said. "But after all this, I guess I've just decided what I've got is worth keeping."

Marcus smiled, as if one of those problems wasn't standing in front of him right now.

"I've just got to convince *her*," he said. "Fair means or foul."

He tapped his lacerated leg. "Maybe I can cage a few months on this. She wouldn't leave me while I'm still laid up. What do you think?"

Colin shook his head noncommittally, as he pushed Marcus' chair to a stop outside his door.

"I'm not exactly the guy to come to," he said. "Most of my relationships end once everybody sobers up."

He shrugged. "Sometimes the old ways are better."

It worked for cavemen, Marcus supposed. A good deal, if you were the alpha male. Marcus was not surprised Colin would think so.

Colin and Marcus regarded each other a moment longer – two rivals, once friends.

Maybe Colin's fiction was better. What good could confrontation do?

Colin patted Marcus on the shoulder as he headed back down the hall – perhaps towards the kitchen – or perhaps the infirmary to see Marcus' wife once before bed.

That had been hours ago. Since then Marcus had been lying there with the ache in his leg like a rotted tooth. As the night ticked on, it only grew worse.

At least the pain provided focus on the here and now. He wouldn't jinx things by thinking *past* the point of a rescue that hadn't happened yet.

As far as his real-world life, nothing had changed, besides the likely addition of thousands in medical bills.

Ridiculously, lying in bed, lizard-bit, shipwrecked on a desert island, Marcus found himself worrying how he was going to earn his living.

Although, *that* issue might go a long way towards solving issues with his wife – who *was* still his *wife*. Which meant he still had time.

He still wanted to make her happy, so she was doing her job. He just had to figure out how to do his.

And if intentions were gold, he'd be a rich man.

The pain in his leg beat like a drum, keeping him in the present, reminding him of more immediate priorities. After all, no one had even called for help yet. Marcus would have expected something by now. He could tell Colin didn't like it. And whatever Colin's status as a rival of the heart, Marcus trusted the man's instincts.

All these things prodded his overstrung nerves, keeping sleep safely at distance.

Finally, Marcus sat up and slid out of bed, setting his foot gingerly on the floor, limping over to the window.

The guest rooms overlooked both the ocean and the rear deck.

Outside his window, the moon had risen, perched perfectly in the middle of its jaunt across the tropical ocean sky.

Down below, the grounds were pitch-black. The lights, he remembered, were motion-activated.

But Marcus knew the dragons were down there, looking up in the dark.

Restless, he stepped out onto the guest-room's small patio, breathing deep in the ocean air. He had been sweating, and the warm breeze actually brought a chilling rash of goose-flesh. He stepped back inside, shutting the door with an unconscious shiver.

Favoring his wounded leg, he made his way to the door. Glancing at the wheelchair in the corner, and with a pulse of stubborn pride, he left it behind as he let himself out into the hallway.

The clock on the wall showed after midnight.

At Marcus' movements, small glow-lights clicked on at his feet, lighting his path.

He saw a light under Mona's room – perhaps she was an insomniac as well.

Colin's light was off – probably sleeping like a baby.

Marcus padded softly past, clinging to the railing that overlooked the main lobby. In the dark, the Gothic tone was even more pronounced – as if the windows had been specifically designed just to play those types of tricks with the light.

The fossil Megalania loomed, display lights highlighting teeth and claws.

Latched onto the rail, favoring his gimpy leg on each deliberate step, Marcus made his way down the circular staircase to the main floor.

Motion-activated lights followed his progress. He also heard a guitar-riff coming from somewhere in the room – a chord from *Stairway to Heaven*.

The overhead lights stayed low, perhaps on a night-mode, letting most of the illumination on the floor come from the displays along the walls.

As Marcus took in the room, he realized that, in the place of the elaborate fish-tanks he had seen in some fancier hotels, Burroughs had placed terrariums. And as he scanned the run of glass-cages, inside were an assortment of lizards, snakes, spiders – even a few large constrictors.

Among them were some pretty scary critters: Taipan, Gaboon Viper, Black Mamba. All among the deadliest in the world.

The display cabinets were lined along the interior perimeter of the building, adjacent to the infirmary. A moment's thought suggested why. It would be where the med-unit would store anti-venom.

He had spent last night in the infirmary only two doors over from the rear access to these cages.

All this, Marcus thought, and Burroughs apparently handled it alone. Any of the animals in those terrariums could cause rapid death. In Marcus' humble opinion, living here alone while interacting among them was insane.

Seriously, how rich did you have to be to live like this? And how *nuts* would you have to be to *want* to?

Marcus hobbled down the hall, the shadows creeping along behind him. As he peered outside, the windows provided a surprisingly clear view, even at night. The specialized glass captured the light like military tac-visors, not just tinting the incoming light, but casting the view of the surrounding countryside in vivid detail.

He could see the pits below.

Something had apparently activated one of the motion sensors, because a series of low, localized lights had popped on. Marcus could see movement as the halfling dragons scattered, suddenly disturbed.

The lights also highlighted that big dragon that sat, vigilant on its perch, along the perimeter fence.

Marcus looked down at his bandaged leg, still seeping blood at the edges. He had been lucky he hadn't severed his Achilles tendon. Probably that indicated an inexperienced lizard. The thing that had latched onto his leg was a relatively little guy.

Not like that big guy on the fence. *That* one would have grown old and sly – not prone to miss strategically-placed bites.

The dragon seemed to be looking at him through the window.

Marcus realized that, right now, he *was* exactly that wounded animal that the predator picked out of the herd. Maybe the thing was picking up on his limp.

Of course, this was also a feeding area. No need to let his imagination run away with him – as he wandered through this gothic mansion in the middle of the night like Scooby-Doo.

Marcus chuckled deliberately, even as he shivered.

The dragon on the fence just watched. Not even bored – just content to wait. Nothing else on its mind.

They didn't care about your human drama. It was all about protein – they didn't care at all if it was you.

Marcus heard another riff in the background – this one Clapton's '*Lay Down Sally*'.

As he turned from the window, he realized the lights in the infirmary were still on.

Was Anna still up? Perhaps kept awake by her own aches and pains? Common ground, at least.

He stood looking at the light emanating from down the hall.

There was so much he didn't want to be so. He hadn't even been able to be her hero. When the opportunity presented itself, he was a bedridden casualty. His biggest contribution had been vacating the infirmary.

Colin, of course, was excruciatingly heroic. And you would have to have been a blind-man not to see how they were together.

Marcus had dutifully wondered if he should just stand aside. Wasn't that the noblest path? It was all about what *she* really wanted – and if he *really* loved her, and all that?

The problem with that was very simple.

He didn't *want* to.

He meant what he told Colin. She was the love of his life and he was going to fight for her.

And no better time than the present. The light in the infirmary waited.

Rapunzel, Rapunzel.

He staggered towards that light like an injured moth. On one hobbled leg, he would bend down on one knee, and ask her to marry him again. Or propose to *stay* married.

He would offer her no rhyme or reason, no describable point of persuasion, other than, *I just want to BE with you.*

For no other reason than that. Forever in blue jeans.

Marcus couldn't think of a single reason for her to say 'yes', but he would ask it nonetheless.

The shadows shifted as the motion-sensors activated the lights, creating the impression of small creatures skittering at the corners. Another musical riff echoed in the empty hall.

Marcus paused, turning back to where the portrait of Lorena Burroughs was enshrined, overlooking the lobby.

The riff sounded again. Gothic ringing bells, leading into AC/DC.

A ringtone.

Marcus blinked and realized that the phone sitting on the desk was ringing – all those auto-dials.

It was receiving calls. Communications were online.

With a lurching, duck-like waddle, Marcus made his way over to the desk and snatched up the phone. He tapped the screen and it came to life. It was not even locked. Why would it be?

The screen gave him a connecting-service message. Marcus hobbled out to the balcony and the clear signal outside.

He actually had a moment of excitement. He was being useful!

Now he would be able to go tell his wife, help was on its way.

'*Him* – not Colin, not Burroughs.

The warm tropical breeze touched his face as he pushed open the balcony doors.

He took a second to savor it – looking out onto the deck, the Olympic pool, the crystal-clear starlit horizon over the ocean – and finally, *finally* he got to save the day.

Marcus smiled. He'd had worse moments.

It never occurred to him to wonder that the motion-activated lights on the deck were already on.

The next thing he heard was a heavy, thudding '*crack*' in the back of his head as he was clubbed from behind.

His world went dark and he dropped bonelessly to the deck.

CHAPTER 28

Marcus was actually knocked *back* awake by sheer impact. And pain.

From blank unconsciousness, suddenly it was as if he'd been thrown into a wall hard enough to literally make him stick.

Then he realized that was his limp body hitting the flat, lava-rock, on the floor of the pit, from a dead drop of better than fifty feet.

The impact was like getting hit by a truck. Marcus felt his right arm break just above the wrist. The rest of him landed more or less flat, distributing the shock evenly – like a giant fly-swatter – possibly adding a few more breaks, but with almost every bone still ringing, it was hard to tell just yet.

His breath was blasted out of him, and he lay gasping like a fish, wondering if he hadn't shattered a few ribs. He felt fresh blood from the ruptured sutures on his leg.

Struggling half-upright with his one good arm, Marcus brayed like a donkey, desperate for air – and at first, he didn't think it was going to come, that he was just too broken, and now he was going to suffocate and die.

With the world spinning, eyes tearing, Marcus gasped an agonized breath.

Motion-activated lights around him kicked on.

When he wiped his eyes clear, he saw the dragons coming for him.

They *scurried* – and Marcus had time to think they were rather like the flocks of ducks he had fed at the lake as a kid – the way they swarmed over the top of each other after a tossed morsel of bread.

And that big bastard was down from the fence, pushing its way up front.

Those weren't the only teeth coming for him, but he got the best look, because those were the ones going for his face.

Marcus found his breath, and let it out in an equally-agonized raking scream.

The dragons fell on him.

He tried to fight, flopping like a seal on one flipper, striking out with his good arm, but doing no damage at all to skin evolved to live around volcanoes. His efforts *did* ignite bolts of pain, alerting the presence of several more broken bones.

Then one of the dragons caught him by his outstretched hand. Almost simultaneously, two others were tearing at his feet and calves.

The teeth were so sharp, he actually felt remarkably little pain, even as he watched his flesh sheared away.

That was the last thing he saw before the big dragon latched onto his face.

Marcus felt the teeth carve into his cheek and neck, and then the splash of wetness as the blood from his severed carotid artery pumped like a burst hose.

His energy faded quickly after that. He made an attempt at a second scream, but only managed a rasp of air out the side of his torn throat.

Incoherently, as the pain begin to fade into confusion, he tried to get up again – not to escape – rising almost half-aware, like getting out of bed – that sub-level of consciousness.

He was getting up to go where he'd been on his way before – up to the infirmary – to see his wife – to ask her to marry him again.

Although, he thought, looking down at himself, as the big dragon pulled away with most of his cheek and lips in its jaws, and the others began to eat him alive – at this point, he *was* kind of damaged goods.

He never even made his feet, unable to even clamber to his knees.

Now he finally collapsed.

Marcus saw that big bastard with a long sleeve of his own face satcheled in its jaws.

With a toss of its head, it swallowed the mouthful.

Then it moved in again.

CHAPTER 29

Mona was not sure what woke her, but she sat up suddenly in bed, out of wind, as if from running. Her heart was hammering and her breath sucked in for a scream.

She blinked awake in the dark, the dream already fading and gone.

After a moment, she lay back in the expensive sheets, letting her pulse slow, and waited to fall back asleep – perhaps rejoin the dream, and find out what had been chasing her.

Minutes passed with unspent adrenaline settling into her system. She finally gave up, sitting up and turning on her light. The wine had left her mouth foul, and she stumbled to the restroom, splashing water over her face.

She took a moment to look at herself, sans-make-up, in the mirror.

Her honest appraisal was that she was still a good-looking woman.

But they weren't making any exceptions for her. She was also seeing the first claws of crowfeet at the corners of her eyes. And she wasn't like Anna – any 'plumpness' she'd acquired since college only threatened to sag-up her figure, and she worked ferociously at the gym to stave it off.

On the plus side, all that exercise made her strong enough to hit a couple of dragons harder than they were expecting.

That was something to put in her personals ad. *Dragon-slayer.*

She technically hadn't actually *slain* any dragons – but 'beat-viciously-with-her-purse' didn't have the same cachet.

She wondered if that was what she had been dreaming about.

Or sharks – can't forget about sharks.

Okay, she decided – no sense trying to sleep anytime soon.

Fortunately, their host was well-stocked in wine.

Donning the five-star robe Burroughs had provided, Mona slipped out into the moon-lit hall.

In the minutes after midnight, the high-tech modern-facility adapted a spooky Old World-ambiance. Mona was actually reminded of the downtown mall, after-hours at Christmas-time – those wee hours after the revelers had gone home, but the early risers still lay in bed, with all those lights, lining buildings and trees, blinking on and off, creating the crawly impression of movement – like the skittering rats in the Nutcracker's tale.

As Mona walked the lonely halls, shadows reached out from the windows like hands, and the solar panels above cast drifting tricks of light upon the floor. A ghost of ventilation tugged like a breeze at her robe.

Mona shivered. Yet, there was a pleasurable quality to it – a feeling of mystery, wandering through an exotic mansion – the setting of one of those old noir-films.

Hollywood played to basics back then. It was an era where actresses were forever helpless damsels in distress, the heroes handsome and brave.

Mona had grown cynical on that last bit.

Of course, what was a cynic, but a wounded dreamer?

Just because she hadn't caught her handsome hero, didn't mean they didn't exist. Colin, for example.

And irony upon irony, she had engineered this whole trip to set him up with someone else.

Granted, that had been while she was concurrently attached. And while one might respectfully expect a bereavement grace-period on her part, based on how *that* ended, Mona felt she could also reasonably throw back an extreme-circumstance exemption-clause.

Besides, Anna and Marcus were both laid up for a while. Forced proximity might actually be the best thing for them – perhaps with Mona's encouraging voice in Anna's ear.

Most importantly, Anna had yet made no direct overtures to Colin, nor specifically said 'divorce'.

Therefore, Mona was going to call 'fair-game'.

The real problem was that Colin was still clearly infatuated with Anna. That long-term devotion was exactly one of the things that made him such a class-act. When he fell, he fell for real.

That did not, however, mean he couldn't move on.

Mona had noted his lights out as he passed his door. She considered knocking anyway, but remembered she hadn't put on make-up.

Maybe *after* the wine.

She padded softly downstairs, noting the lights in the lobby blinking in that Christmas-department-store fashion.

The lights were also on in the infirmary down the hall, she realized. Was Anna still up?

Or, she wondered, was that why Colin's room was dark?

Mona paused.

Wine first, she thought.

The kitchen bordered the rear deck, opening into a fancy restaurant-style dining room. Mr. Burroughs spared no expense. Lorena Burroughs would have likely had any physical possession she desired – albeit in an isolated, zombie-apocalypse kind of way.

Take away the pit full of dragons, you could almost sell her on it.

Unfortunately, the lizards seemed part of the package.

Still, the view from the deck was majestic. Mona stopped, her slim shadow dwarfed by the panoramic picture window, that led out to the pool.

A crystal-stark backdrop of stars framed the moon. She felt a small chill, realizing she was probably one of the only people in the world seeing this view.

The isolation was humbling. But in a way, it was its own blessing, as if the starscape was there just for her.

Eventually, she would be home again, and she would want to remember this moment after it was long gone.

She stopped a moment to take it all in.

As she did so, she noticed movement on the deck.

The lights were on outside. For the first time, that struck her as odd – the lights were motion-activated.

And now, she realized, the doors were standing open.

Out on the deck, someone was carrying Marcus over one shoulder.

Marcus was unconscious, but Mona could tell it was him by the bed-clothes he'd worn in the infirmary. The other figure was back to her, and as they stepped up to the guard rail beneath the glare of the lights, all Mona could see was a shadow.

As Mona watched, thunderstruck, the figure leaned over and, with a Neanderthal-caveman grunt, pitched Marcus over the railing.

The unconscious body fell loosely, like a sack of sand, bouncing awkwardly off the rail, and there was a muffled curse – "Owww, *shit!*" – as the person – the *killer* – evidently smacked their hand, as they threw Marcus over.

There was a dizzying pause and then the sickening thump of meat hitting the volcanic rock below.

Mona sucked a chirp of breath, holding back a scream.

The figure at the railing stared down over the edge, watching.

From below, there came the first reedy shrieks, as if from someone with broken ribs and punctured lungs trying to scream.

Mona froze, standing exposed in the middle of the hall, afraid to move. She glanced back towards the infirmary. Or should she try to make it across the lobby upstairs – wake up Colin?

Unless, he was already in the infirmary with Anna.

Mona faded back to the shadows, and promptly knocked her arm hard against a protruding shelf. She smothered a yelp of pain as the figure on the deck paused at the sound.

Clinging to the wall, Mona edged through the lobby until she reached the hallway to the infirmary and started to run.

Her head was spinning. What was she supposed to do? She'd just seen a man murdered.

And what was she going to tell Anna?

But as she rounded the corner, she realized the door to the infirmary was standing open, and the curtains on the windows were closed.

Mona caught her breath. What if something had happened?

She heard voices. When she looked in through the open door, Anna was sitting up in bed.

Richard Burroughs was sitting in a chair beside her, with a cup of coffee, legs folded, in the manner of one reciting old tales. They both looked up, surprised, as Mona stumbled through the door.

"Ah, Mrs. Watson," Burroughs said amiably. "Can't sleep either?"

But then they saw her face.

Anna's eyes widened. "Mona? What's wrong?"

Burroughs was rising from his chair. "Mrs. Watson...?"

Mona looked between the two of them.

"It's Marcus...," she began helplessly.

Her voice choked.

"Someone's in the house. Someone threw him over the balcony."

Tears began to fall down her cheeks, and she wasn't sure if it was more grief or fear.

"Oh, honey... I think he was dead."

CHAPTER 30

Anna shook her head – reflexive rejection, as if she had misunderstood, or was being put on.

On sheer etiquette, you simply didn't just walk in and *say* something like that and have it be real.

But Mona knelt by her bed, taking her hand – squeezing it so she would *know*.

Marcus had been Anna's husband for ten years. Mona recalled some of her own words to him in recent days. 'Low-rent' she had called him.

"I'm so sorry, honey."

Burroughs was standing at the door, looking out at the empty hall.

Anna was still struggling with the affront to her sense of rationality.

A couple of minutes ago, things were fine. Therefore, this simply couldn't be.

In an absent way, it occurred to her that she had been right before – Taylor *had* been somewhere close.

Now she wondered what he had in mind for the rest of them.

He said he needed a mate. He'd made it a joke. But he said it twice. He also freely acknowledged that he no longer felt sane.

Had he now just murdered her husband? A caveman taking out the competing male?

"He's been shot," Burroughs said, grimly, "And he's already quite deranged."

Mona looked nervously at the infirmary's open door.

"What do we do? It's just *us*. He's still out there."

"Well," Burroughs said, "if you ladies wouldn't mind waiting here for a moment..."

He stepped out into the hall, moving quickly, disappearing around the corner, only to appear less than a minute later, cradling a rifle.

"Mrs. Watson, if you would please show me where Mr. Miller fell."

Anna sat up in bed. "Wait a minute. You're not leaving me alone. Mona, you stay right here."

Burroughs paused.

"He couldn't have come this way without us seeing him," he said. "But perhaps you're right. I should get you a gun."

"I don't want a *gun*!" Anna said.

"Uh," Mona said, interjecting, "*I'll* take a gun."

Burroughs nodded. "Come with me. I'll get you something out of the cabinet. You can come back here with Mrs. Miller. I think it's time to wake Captain Braddock. Then the two of us can deal with Mr. Taylor."

Mona squeezed Anna's hand reassuringly, standing up. "I'll be right back."

Anna stared back unhappily.

Mona knew she was no less safe following Burroughs into the hallway than hiding in the infirmary – probably safer with Burroughs' rifle – but she nevertheless felt her confidence evaporating. She crowded close to Burroughs, who adapted the posture of a man on a hunt.

The curve of the hall opened the view of the lobby by degrees. The motion-activated lights were still on.

The Megalania smiled a toothy greeting as the two of them stepped cautiously into the lobby.

Then a voice sounded from the level above, eliciting a small screech from Mona.

"Hey!" Colin hollered, looking down from the balcony, rubbing sleep out of his eyes, "what the hell is everybody doing up?"

Then he saw Burroughs' rifle.

"What's the ruckus?"

"I'm glad you're up, Captain," Burroughs said. "We might be needing you."

Colin came downstairs, raising his eyes as Burroughs rifled through his gun cabinet, turning to hand him back his same 30.06 from before.

Colin took the rifle. "No perfume this time?"

"These are not for the dragons, Captain Braddock," Burroughs said.

Mona was again struck as the rather doddering old fop squared his shoulders, and now gave the impression of a man who was self-sufficient and coarse – who didn't move slowly, but never wasted a motion, and who had learned to physically interact with dangerous animals far stronger than humans – a man who could rough it and survive in the jungle.

The look in his eyes was purposeful, and no longer gentle.

Burroughs handed Mona a 9mm pistol.

"Here," he said. He tapped the small button on the side. "That's the safety. It is now *on*. Turn it off to fire. You have nine shots. It's semi-automatic, so you simply aim and pull the trigger. Can you do that?"

Three days ago, Mona would have said, *no way*. But that was before she'd seen her boyfriend eaten by a shark, and before she had beaten a Komodo monitor off of her best-friend's husband's leg with her purse. And certainly before she'd seen him thrown over a ledge to be eaten alive.

"I can do that," she said.

'Then, Mrs. Watson, if you would please show us where you saw Mr. Miller fall?"

Colin's ears perked.

"Someone mind telling me what's going on?"

"It seems your friend Mr. Miller has been murdered, Captain," Burroughs said. "And we believe Mr. Taylor is loose somewhere on the property."

Colin frowned. He shouldered his rifle.

"Okay," he said.

It was dark on the main deck, but the lights switched on again once they stepped out on the veranda, sequenced to resemble torches catching fire, racing to the end of the pool. A clever illusion – the sort of thing wealth could do on a whim.

Mona pointed to the southeast railing.

"There," she said.

Colin held back, scouting the deck. The space was open and visible. Even the pool water glowed blue and clear.

There were, however, lights on below – down in the pit.

Activity.

Burroughs leaned over the railing, looking down.

And for some reason, she would never know why, knowing full well what she was likely to see, Mona looked over as well.

It had been maybe twenty minutes since Marcus had fallen.

The dragons had torn him apart – stomach first – his entrails were strung out, and the lizards fought and tugged jealously, battling for their share, but also working together to tear the carcass apart.

The major organs had already been hollowed out, but still they fought their way in for more, even as the others began tearing at his arms and legs.

His face was torn away below the cheeks, but Mona could see his dead eyes. His head bobbed as his body was wrenched back and forth.

There looked to be a smashed cell-phone lying in the lava-rock beside him.

One of the dragons took notice of the audience to their unexpected midnight feast, and looked up, expectantly, lips bloody, greedy for more.

Marcus, Mona realized, was not the first to go over that railing.

She felt her stomach lurch. No one deserved this.

Burroughs hit a switch – one of many that looked like decorative buttons along the railing posts. There was the sound of gas, and the scent of Hot Kitty drifted up from below.

The lizards scattered from the body.

Marcus looked like a stuffed animal that had been split open and its stuffing spread, with his head still hanging loose.

"I think I'm going to be sick," Mona muttered, turning away.

Colin stepped up beside her and looked over the railing.

"Awww *shit*," he said.

And Mona's ears perked.

She turned.

Awww *shit*.

Owww *shit.*

It was the exact same cadence. The same inflection.

That was why they had suspects in line-ups repeat sentences.

Colin was grimacing at the scene below.

"Poor bastard," he said, shaking his head, turning away. Then he saw the look on Mona's face.

"Hey," he said. "Are you alright?"

He reached to steady her.

Mona, however, backed away from his outstretched hand.

She was looking at the scrape across the knuckles – just the sort you might get against a marble railing.

"You're bleeding," she said. "What happened to your hand?"

She looked into his eyes. It was a moment of pure communication between them.

"Boy," Colin said, "I really wish you hadn't figured that out."

Mona was holding a nine-millimeter in her hands – for all the good it did her. Colin stepped forward and struck her across the face with the butt of his rifle.

Mona dropped bonelessly. The blow itself was probably enough to kill her. The pistol clattered where she dropped it on the deck.

Burroughs turned to face Colin's raised rifle.

"Set your gun down, Mr. Burroughs."

Burroughs leaned his rifle against the railing and stepped away. Colin took it, slinging the strap over one shoulder. Then he grabbed up Mona's loose pistol and stuffed it in his belt.

He looked down at Mona's motionless body.

"For what it's worth," he said, "I'm sorry about this."

But then he shrugged.

"On the other hand, I never much liked you anyway."

With that, he bent to pick her up, and tossed her over the railing.

There was a brief pause, followed by impact – not quite so heavy as before.

This time, however, the scream came from behind him.

Colin and Burroughs both turned to find Anna standing at the door.

CHAPTER 31

Anna stood frozen, her scream still echoing between the open deck and the empty Gothic halls.

She had seen Mona's limp, probably already lifeless body flip over the railing. She heard the thump of meat hitting below. There had been no accompanying scream.

Anna had maybe half-a-second to marvel at how different the world might have been if she had just obediently stayed where she was. Even a couple of minutes would have made the difference between what she would have believed versus what she would have *known*.

Of course, Marcus, if he'd still been alive, could have told anyone there Anna wasn't going to stay put.

It was that stubborn streak in her. Ironically, she never seemed able to resist when it kicked in active, as if her normal personality was so passive that when her assertive shadow put its foot down, she just proceeded on unfettered impulse.

Sitting there in the infirmary, she had realized she felt fine. Taylor might be crazy, but whatever shot he'd given her – probably penicillin, and *yes*, she sort of remembered him asking in passing if she was allergic before he jabbed her in the ass – the salient point was that it had worked. She was not badly injured and was finally well-rested.

She had also just been told her husband was dead.

Her mind was currently operating on a sort of stand-by state of shock.

She wasn't quite ready to believe it – and therefore, she was not yet quite sure how to react.

And sitting there waiting was going to drive her purely and simply crazy.

Anna decided she wasn't going to. *This* Jane had now made it through the jungle. She could handle a spooky mansion.

Better to stay active and moving – otherwise, her idle mind might threaten to contemplate the future.

Any life-decisions she had been agonizing over, might very well have become moot – and even mundane.

It all seemed so embarrassingly petty to her now.

She'd come all the way around the world to live out a girlish fantasy – to give Colin another chance to ask a question she'd said 'no' to, ten years before. And hadn't she just been delighted to find the chemistry between them unchanged, as if they'd continued to know each other all along?

But... not like *this*. She wouldn't be able to live with herself.

She had to know. She had to know for sure, so she could know how to *feel*.

Anna pushed cautiously out into the hall. She had not toured the building, beyond simply being carried up from the garage, but she followed the path of lights.

The low-glow illumination rising *up* from the floor was eerie, almost elvish. The motion-activated bulbs followed your movements, and played constant tricks with the shadows – which themselves were morphed and twisted by the filter of solar panels lining the roof. A bizarre sort of energy efficiency, that conspired to preserve the Gothic decor at night.

And the silken, sad, uncertain rustling of each purple curtain...

The old verse echoed silently in her head.

... thrilled me, filled me, with fantastic terrors never felt before.

When she had come out into the main lobby, the lights on the outside deck stood out.

She had walked up on them.

Seconds would have made the difference. But she had seen enough.

Colin met her eyes nakedly.

But everything she knew about him for ten years, was now filtered through the prism of what she had known for ten seconds.

A thousand thoughts, a thousand considerations – *ten years spent pining* – an imagination run wild on schoolgirl fantasies.

She was cured of THAT if nothing else.

Even if it might be a bit late in the game.

Colin stepped forward, reaching out.

Anna backed up.

"Stay where you are," she warned.

Warned. She almost snickered. *As if.*

Colin held up a placating hand. "Okay."

He looked at her helplessly. "Anna, listen..."

And while he was trying to speak, Anna closed and locked the heavy glass doors in front of him.

Colin realized it a second too late. "Shit!" he barked, rushing forward, just as the lock snapped shut.

Anna stood a moment, staring through the glass. Then she turned to run.

She was alone, she realized – utterly alone.

And there was nowhere to go.

She ran past the grinning Megalania, hunting for Burroughs' gun-cabinet – but then a shot rang out, shattering the glass door, and Colin's voice echoed into the lobby.

"*Anna?*"

Moving against the wall, keeping to the shadows, Anna slipped around to the access stairway that led down to the lower levels.

And then what? After that, was outside. She would be barefoot, draped in a paper-thin hospital smock, over the same damned bikini she'd been moldering in for three days.

The stairway's motion-activated lights lit up her path in that creepy, post-midnight, time-saver, electric-candlelight.

Which, she realized, announced her presence, as surely as if the house itself was deliberately, malevolently flushing her out.

Sure enough, she heard Colin on the stairs behind her.

For a hair-brained moment, she considered attempting some kind of ambush. But the thought of *her* trying to take down Colin with anything short of a gun was laughable.

"Anna?" he called again. "Please... I'm not going to hurt you."

Anna didn't slow. As if.

The lights in the stairway lit up in front of her, all the way down to the garage – the access-way to the bridge – but Anna paused. The other option was to find someplace to hide.

She looked around at the unappealing nooks and crannies, nestled between breeding labs and incubation chambers – all full of caged dragons. Some of the skittering little devils were no bigger than rats, their eyes popping interestedly as a person passed by, hopeful for the tidbits of food they'd come to expect.

Anna felt along the wall, marking Colin's advancing shadow down the stairs. Then her reaching hand stumbled on the wall switch. Switching to manual override, Anna punched the lights.

In an instant, the lower levels were draped in inky black, made all the more stark by the continued, steady glow of terrariums, obviously on a stored power-charge. Even the tac-visor-tinted windows were shadows.

Anna ducked into the smallest corner she could find. If just by chance, she could feint him down to the garage, she *might* be able to lock him out of the house.

"*Oh, for...*" Colin let out an irritated mutter.

There was a flash as he struck a match, holding it cupped in his hands. "I guess this means you're over by the light switch," he said.

Anna froze. She hadn't thought of that.

Now she was trapped. The only exit on this level was the stairs themselves.

And the only thing behind her was the open deck that led to the main feeding station.

Colin shook out the match. Then she heard his hands rapping along the wall, hunting for the switch, and a moment later, the lights blinked back on.

Anna sat crouched in full-view at the feeding-bay door.

Colin turned towards her, slowly and gently, but still cutting off her retreat.

"Anna..."

Anna slipped outside the door, out onto the feeding deck, turned and pushed the door shut behind her. She couldn't find a lock – which was probably on the inside – so she braced the door with her foot.

Standing just inside the glass, Colin rolled his eyes, his patience fading.

He leaned his shoulder into the door and pushed steadily – not shoving and possibly dragging the door over her feet – but simply applying force superior to hers until she fell back.

He stood in the doorway, not yet angry, but reaching for her more assertively.

His face went utterly slack as Anna tossed her legs over the railing and dropped off over the side.

They were another level down from the pool-deck, and deeper into the upward slope of the cliff, but it was still a good thirty-foot drop, and it *hurt* when Anna landed barefoot on the flat, broken volcanic rock.

But even though she hadn't practiced in years, Anna had grown up with the reflexes of a gymnast. She absorbed the shock in her legs and rolled.

The impact still knocked out her wind, and she lay for a moment, stunned, before she even began to gasp for air. The movement caused the overhead lights to blink on, blinding her.

As her eyes adjusted, the first thing she saw was what was left of Marcus.

It wasn't much. They'd been at him for half-an-hour – and there were a lot of them, piled on, grubbing for every last bit.

She only knew him because of his clothes. And the ring still on his outstretched hand.

Mona was more recognizable. She had landed face-first on the volcanic rock, but the dragons had rolled her over to get at the soft flesh of her stomach, spreading out the contents.

The big dragon from the fence had assumed dominant position at the head of the table, reaping the rewards of its patient vigil. The others tore at Mona's arms and legs, jerking and fighting, desperate to gorge before the pickings were gone.

Anna saw a couple of the smaller dragons, perhaps chased off the main feast, now perked in her direction.

Colin shouted down from the railing.

"Jesus! *Anna!*"

She had made it to her hands and knees, and was struggling with her first breaths, as the dragons started towards her.

Then she heard the hissing of gas, and smelled the cloying scent of Hot Kitty. The dragons scattered.

All except the sentry from the fence. It held its position on Mona's corpse, now eyeing Anna curiously.

This particular dragon had learned not to fear Hot Kitty.

Now why might *that* be?

There was another spitting hiss and Anna caught the first acid whiff of tear-gas.

Now the big dragon retreated, skittering across the yard, and scaling the twenty-foot wall opposite the bridge in bare seconds.

But it stopped there, holding its post.

"*Anna*," Colin shouted again. "Hang on! I'm coming down!"

Looking up into the light, Anna couldn't see what he was doing – likely rigging up a rope or ladder of some kind.

For the moment, the way to the rear fence was clear.

The bridge was twelve feet at its lowest point, right where it joined the pit wall – a jump like that would take a trained gymnast with eight years of dance team through high school and college.

Anna got a running start and ran up the side of the pit wall as if she intended to simply keep going. The moment her momentum faded, she pushed off and hurdled herself upwards.

Her reaching fingers caught the lowest hanging rail. The moment her grip caught, her second hand joined it, and then she flipped her legs overhead, and clambered up onto the bridge.

She looked back to the house, where Colin stared after her from the dock.

Anna turned, scaling the fence like a wood-nymph, and took off running into the forest.

CHAPTER 32

How different it was this time, in the dark.

The last time she'd fled through this forest, it had been towards the hope of some imagined salvation. Now, there *was* no safe-haven.

Anna stuck to the main path, which allowed her to stretch into a run, her short-term goal simply to create distance.

She also wanted to keep moving, lest any lingering dragons catch her scent. If she could make it to the coast, she could travel along the bare cliff, where the visibility was higher.

Beyond that, Anna had no idea.

The dragons were everywhere. It didn't matter where she went, as soon as she settled down in any one place, her scent would carry, and they would follow.

Although, there was the possible option of Taylor's cave.

Under hasty reevaluation, she now realized the last time she had seen him, he'd been shot – and *could* very likely be dead. All her earlier vapors about him lurking about, stalking her, were pure projection. Reality had insinuated its sobering face.

But if Taylor was gone, that meant he'd left behind supplies in his cave.

Unfortunately, she had coughed *all* that up to Burroughs. Anna had no doubt Colin would get *that* much out of him.

That left a finite window. Again, assuming Taylor himself wasn't waiting for her when she got there.

Great plan so far. Given no options.

Anna listened for the sound of pursuit. If she heard a vehicle engine, she would have to ditch the path into the brush and whatever might be waiting there.

And as if her very thought had conjured it, she caught movement in the bushes, just after she flashed past, as if belatedly flushing a pheasant.

Anna paused, turning to see what, out of any number of possible horrors might emerge. It didn't even *have* to be a dragon – there was a whole cast of creepy-crawlies. Spiders, foot-long centipedes. *And* snakes. She'd already gotten a really good look at a cobra.

It was no cobra, however, that popped its head up above the long grass behind her, followed by the dorsal-like lashing tail, its owner apparently roused too-late, as Anna streaked by its ambush.

But now it stepped out into the path behind her.

This dragon was BIG. Far and away the largest she'd seen on the island – *easily* twice the girth of that big bastard on the fence – the one that she had left with part of her husband's face in its teeth.

Anna didn't know record sizes for Komodo dragons, but she recognized abnormal when she saw it. She wondered what Burroughs had been giving them. There was raising animals for conservation, and then there was pumping beef cattle full of hormones.

It seemed unlikely that nature alone had created *this* monster.

The dragon regarded her studiously, gauging distance, tongue scenting the air – no doubt picking up on all that Hot Kitty.

Was she close enough to make a rush, perhaps?

But no, after a judicial pause, it instead simply lurch-stepped into that slow, methodical, hand-over-hand plod.

Just walking – an ambling afterthought, moseying in her general direction. Anna could see the massive claws flex as it moved.

And no doubt there were more dragons lurking in the bushes beyond – perhaps giving *this* beast a respectful range – but they were there sure enough.

Every time she looked, there would be a few more of them. If she ran, when she looked again, they would somehow be closer than before.

Soon enough, she would have to sleep. But they never slept. They just sort of... stopped for a while, sometimes running off into the shade or a mud-hole. Then they got up and kept going – no wasted motion – that scent-tracking tongue leading them unerringly, implacably, forward until they finally found you unguarded.

Caveman Taylor's solution was to eat one and then use its teeth as a spear to kill the next.

Respect is earned.

And yet, every morning for five years, the dragons had still been there, in the trees, on the beach, hiding in the rocks, just out of sight in the dark.

Five years, Taylor had been alone. Night after night, days into years. Would you even remember what civilized life was like?

She looked back at the prehistoric monster advancing down the path behind her.

Taking Taylor's example, she found herself a thick branch, a stiff-length that looked as if it might have been cleared when the path was cut, and was now a dried and sharpened husk.

Anna spent a moment, peeling away the extraneous branches.

The dragon ambled ever-closer, its head bobbing back and forth, clearly unconcerned.

As she shouldered her makeshift dragon-lance, Anna actually found herself smiling. One of her most treasured DVDs as a child was the first season of *Land of the Lost* – where one of the lost family's daily chores had been to poke 'Grumpy' the *T. rex* in the throat with a phone-pole-sized log as it snarled into the mouth of their cave. And then they would play tag with the beast as they gathered their lunch of giant strawberries, the big tyrannosaur chasing them back and forth.

Anna eyed the dragon, and its leisurely pursuit. Once they got on your tail, Taylor had told her, they stayed there until they got you.

"Okay, Grumpy," Anna said, "you're *it.*"

Anna turned, stepping up into a run.

Unhurried, the dragon followed.

CHAPTER 33

Colin informed Burroughs at gunpoint that he would be helping to find Anna. Burroughs acquiesced agreeably enough, and led them down to the garage.

"If she's smart," he said, "she'll travel the coast. That's the easiest terrain."

"Well, then," Colin said, motioning with his rifle, "*you* drive."

Burroughs smiled easily, cranking the Jeep to life, and activated the garage remote...

... and they sat there waiting as the door open inexorably *slowly*, as if on purpose.

Colin grit his teeth. Burroughs' mild grin broadened ever so slightly, as he nudged the Jeep out on the bridge, so they could again wait for the slow mechanics of the main gate – which again kicked and stopped at that same spot, pausing a couple of minutes this time before it started up again.

In those minutes, Burroughs was already going to work on Colin's last nerves.

Colin knew it, and reminded himself that he was emotionally involved.

The gate finally rolled open, and Burroughs – perhaps just a half-second slower than he had to – pulled forward out onto the dirt road.

Colin had seen Anna take off down the path.

They *had* to find her. She'd been lucky last night – she'd had a guardian.

But by herself in these woods at night?

Colin pushed the thought aside. He did it deliberately and professionally, the way he always did, when action was called for. Don't let the *facts* of the situation block you from *dealing* with it.

That also meant *not* thinking about what came next. Those were things that would have to be dealt with later.

Burroughs, however, wasn't having it.

"Exactly what do you think is going to happen?" he asked, as he bounced the Jeep slowly along. "You don't seriously think she's going to come back with you?"

Colin took a patient breath.

"It doesn't matter. She'll be killed out there alone."

"I'm not saying you're wrong," Burroughs said mildly. "But I *am* letting you know you're going to have to physically overpower her and drag her in restraints back to the compound."

"I am prepared to do that," Colin said.

"I have no doubt," Burroughs replied, amiably. "Don't misunderstand. I don't judge you. You're simply behaving like a primal male. Eliminating competition to secure a mate. It's one of those things all creatures great and small fight over. After food and territory, it's always about mating rights. The third corner of nature's Trinity.

"But," he said, eyeing Colin meaningfully, "*I'm* not the problem, am I?"

Burroughs switched into four-wheel, flicking on the Jeep's brights, illuminating the path through the trees. He touched the remote, and behind them, the ponderously slow garage door began to roll shut, like a slow-motion trapdoor over the mouth of a cave. There was the sound of shifting gears and the main gate started to slide shut as well.

"The problem," Burroughs said, "is that she saw the *real* you."

Colin didn't answer, not rising to it. But Burroughs smiled knowingly.

"She liked your rough edges. A small-city girl, like that. She sensed the *beast* in you.   Pure animal attraction.   On short acquaintance, I'm quite sure, that's exactly what drew her. Especially after meeting her husband."

Burroughs laughed. "Socio-sexual-psychology. It hurts the tongue just to say. Which really makes it all much more complicated than it needs to be. When you get down to it, it's all very simple.

"In this case," he said, "it's the difference between sensing and seeing. She caught the beast in the act of *being* a beast. And now she fears you."

Colin shut his eyes. The old man wasn't wrong.

He wasn't going to shut up about it, either.

"If you'd gotten away with it, she would have likely been blissfully, even willfully unaware. But I'm afraid you have burst her bubble. The magic-dust, as they say, has rubbed off."

Burroughs shook his head sadly.

"That's forever," he said. "And you know it."

Colin let out a slow breath, turning Burroughs a cold speculative eye. The old man caught the look, and his smile broadened.

"Thinking about killing me too? I'm guessing that was on your short-term menu back there on the pool deck. I'd be your third murder tonight. It gets easy fast, doesn't it?"

Colin settled uncomfortably in his seat. Again, the old man wasn't wrong.

Burroughs chuckled, unworried.

"Like I said, Captain, I'm not judging you. It's nature. It's ALPHA. The noble lion will take over harems of females, killing its predecessor, ripping the genitalia off rivals, and killing the cubs to make way for his own.

"I'll bet your Anna loves lions," Burroughs said. "I bet she loves all big cats. I'll bet she thinks they're *beautiful*.

"Except," he said, "*this* lion murdered her husband. *And* her best friend. Right in front of her. And she actually got to see the revolting half-eaten corpse. *That's* an image that's not going to fade over time."

Colin shut his eyes. Again – not wrong.

"So," Burroughs continued, "now you go out to save her anyway. Because you love her. But what then, Captain?"

Colin said nothing. The truth was, he didn't know.

For the first time in a long, long while, he was genuinely frightened.

There was only one other night in his life he could remember being this afraid.

Funny that it involved a lot of the same people.

It was the night he had left UCLA and the States behind, forever – the night he had proposed to Anna.

He had never told anyone *why* he left that night.

It was not because Anna had said 'no'. It was because, after she said it, he had gone over to the frat where he and Marcus were members, where he happened to know Marcus was partying it up that night. It was the end of a big mid-term week, and the fraternity was throwing a kegger – the lot of them carrying on like a bunch of drunken louts.

The house ran over a modest crick. Frat legend was that more than one drunken reveler had managed to drown in the water under the bridge. There was even a ghost story.

Colin had gone there that night intending to add one more.

He had been leaning in the crook of a tree, half-a-block away, as the party peaked, and wound down into the after-hours – watching for Marcus, who would soon be walking home to the apartment they shared.

Somewhere after three-o'clock, the last stereo finally faded as the last of the hard-drinkers passed out.

Standing out in the cold snap of early spring air, Colin had been struck with a moment of clarity.

What in God's name am I doing?

Suddenly, he had felt glaringly naked and exposed. The realization of what he had really, actively been thinking rose up in a moment of horrified shame and cold terror.

And so he had fled. He ran home to their apartment, grabbed his passport and a duffel, and he had left town. He sent for his stuff, and accepted Incompletes in all of his classes.

The difference between then and tonight had been opportunity and impulse.

There had been no time for a moment of clarity to intercede.

And boy, hadn't things escalated quickly?

"Well, Captain?" Burroughs said. "What's next after your heroic rescue? And what do you think Mrs. Miller will have to say to the authorities?"

At that, Colin turned.

"I'm going to guess," he said, "that the authorities have not yet been notified, have they?"

Burroughs patted his vest pocket. "Left my phone back at the house." He smiled. "So, Captain, if that's your question, you *can* factor into your decisions that no one in the outside world knows you're here."

Colin took a deep breath, his patience drawing thin.

"Tell you what, Mr. Burroughs," he said. "Let's just get Anna back safe. If you help me do that, I might get talked into not killing you. You let me worry about the rest. How's that?"

Burroughs nodded agreeably, throwing one arm casually on the window as he drove.

"You know," Colin said, "I wonder why I get the feeling I'm not the only one who's thrown someone over that balcony?"

"What are you suggesting, Captain?"

"I think you want to keep what happened to your wife private."

"Perhaps. Maybe because what happened was not quite an accident. And maybe there's a man I blame for her death still living on this island. A man who I have yet to definitively settle with."

"And a woman who looks like your cheating wife," Colin said.

Burroughs raised his brows. "What are you getting at, Captain?"

Colin glared. "Just shut up and drive."

The Jeep bumped along, the headlight beams bouncing over the foliage ahead.

Behind them, as the gate dragged slowly closed, a shaggy figure slipped out of the brush.

Taylor looked after the retreating taillights, before he ran for the gate, slipping through as it rolled shut.

CHAPTER 34

It had been five years since Taylor stood inside the compound.

As the garage door trundled shut behind him, he felt oddly skittish – oddly feral, an animal wary of a human dwelling at night.

He had bled the last time he was here too.

Anna had streaked past him on the trail, but in his current condition, there was no way he was going to catch her at a flat run. The lady was surprisingly fast.

Taylor had, however, come loaded for bear. He had a duffel full of bleach, gasoline, perfume, and over his shoulder, he carried a really big, sharp stick.

It was likely to be his last stand, after all. Based on the hole in his gut, Burroughs had finally bagged him. Might as well make the walk in full dress.

There was a surreal quality to looking down at yourself and seeing a hole blown through the middle of you, clean out the back. Blood seeped where he had duct-taped himself.

Taylor was an animal-medic, but anatomy was anatomy, and shot was shot. He would have to be going forward on the assumption that he would not be alive in another few hours.

He briefly thought of trying to call for help, even making the perfunctory effort to log in to one of Burroughs' lab screens.

But of course, all communications had been locked.

Burroughs wouldn't have wanted any of the castaways getting off the island by accident.

Taylor also briefly considered the infirmary. But what was the point? What was he going to do? Perform surgery on himself?

The stairs were slippery with his blood as he made his way up to the main lobby.

Megalania greeted him, its prehistoric fangs and claws posed in a frozen attack.

Taylor stopped, regarding the prehistoric beast, thankfully a million years dead.

He used to *like* this thing. It made it worse, somehow – when the things you once loved became your poison.

He did what he'd learned to do. He stopped caring.

Then he found the portrait of Lorena Burroughs mounted on the wall. *That* was new. It was the first time he'd seen her face in five years.

Taylor choked once, a brief hiccup, before locking it all back down again.

He loved her.

It was the first time he admitted it, even to himself.

There was one moment – the barest second – where she might have known it.

If so, she had been severely punished for it.

Taylor shut his eyes. He had believed himself numb.

He was wrong.

Five years welled up inside, all at once. Anyone watching would have thought he was having a stroke – he froze in place, his hand over his eyes, just waiting to see if the pain would simply overwhelm him.

His fail-safe wasn't working – he couldn't not care.

So instead he just had to suck it up and live with it.

Pain was a just memory in his mind – the actual injury was years done.

There *was* a plan, however, he'd had in mind for a long time – something he'd dreamed over and over, if he *ever* got the opportunity.

The outer walls of the compound were variously marble, glass, and steel. But the interior would burn just fine.

Taylor had learned to be efficient with gas and fire. He torched the curtains and the walls, carpets and furniture, methodically setting it all ablaze.

On the next level, he torched the labs, which were just *full* of combustibles, and he pointedly made no effort to free Burroughs' breeding stock from their cages.

He wanted something that would *hurt*.

The fire was catching nicely as Taylor spread it the rest of the way down to the garage, and to each vehicle, one at a time – save for one last four-wheeling dune-buggy.

There were also several sealed gas-tanks, oil cans, and general maintenance chemicals that should blow sky high, once the flames reached them.

Smoke was filling the room and flames were licking precariously at his shoulders as he started up the remaining four-wheeler.

As he pulled out onto the bridge, he stopped briefly, looking back over his shoulder at the burning compound.

The windows had taken an interior glow, like a jack o-lantern, the tactical glass playing with the light.

Taylor was tempted to watch it burn. But then he looked down at his gut, reminding himself he was on a finite schedule.

He shifted the four-wheeler into gear.

"Now *you*, Mr. Burroughs," he said.

CHAPTER 35

Anna heard the Jeep engine behind her, signaling pursuit. She stopped, looking back, debating what options were left.

At least she could out-sprint a lizard. She had left the big dragon some distance behind – it had made no particular effort to press the chase, simply following along in its own good time.

There was a presumption of superiority in its reptilian attitude – ironic, because Anna had always thought of mammals as the more advanced evolutionary form – the new warm-blooded model replacing the outdated cold-bloods. But one of the upgrades of the endotherm was supposedly stamina. Yet, in this war of attrition, she was the one who would need to rest. If she could not find safe refuge, this obsolete ectotherm would simply chase her down in slow-motion – over several days if necessary.

And once THAT thing got its teeth in her... well, it wouldn't be a matter of bleeding out. The beast was damn near the size of a tiger. It would just tear her apart.

So she ran, quickly leaving the giant monitor behind and out of sight. She ran until the manicured road ended and the coast broke off into the ocean.

The path behind her was still empty, but she knew it was an illusion. The dragon was still on her tail, perhaps following just around the turn – or more likely, simply cutting right through the brush in a straight line.

More problematically, she now saw the headlights illuminating the trees.

Colin had seen her run down the path and knew her only possible route was along the cliffs that enveloped the coast.

Anna didn't see an 'out'. They were going to catch her. Or the dragons would.

She was stubborn, though, and intended to keep running until they ran her down. She took off along the precipice at a slow jog, looking for the first break in the foliage.

When she saw the lights of the Jeep pull out onto the road behind her, Anna cut into the brush.

Now she was operating on blind faith, mindful of her bare feet as she stumbled her way through the long grass, and simply trusting that something with teeth, claws, or venom, wasn't hiding behind every blade.

The Jeep pulled up to the gap in the trees.

She threw herself to the ground, peering through the grass.

The Jeep paused and a spotlight passed over her head. She heard Colin's voice.

"Anna?"

The light scanned the trees slowly.

Finally the light beam receded and the Jeep began rolling again. Anna could hear the crunch of volcanic gravel as they continued south down the coast.

That had been her escape route.

But then she stopped, turning to look back, in realization.

Had they just left her an open path back to the compound?

It occurred to her *that* might be a lot better place to hide, particularly if she could find some way to barricade them out, while they were out in the woods looking for her.

Certainly better than some smelly old cave.

Anna rose to her feet, keeping an eye on the retreating Jeep, as she waded back out of the long grass.

Standing in the middle of the road, waiting patiently, was the dragon.

Its head perked as it saw her, its tongue lolling out, just to taste her on the air.

And apparently deciding its target was finally sufficiently in-range for the expense of energy, the beast broke into a run.

No slow, ambling plod this time, the creature almost seemed to explode into movement – the skittering speed of a lizard on an animal the size of a tiger, its massive forelimbs rowing hand-over-hand, the claws flaring as they caught the ground and launched the monster-beast forward.

Anna screamed, a purely involuntary, guttural expulsion of terror.

She turned to run. It was an open glade of tall grass, which was obviously why the dragon picked it – a prey animal would have no cover. The strategy of instinct.

Anna realized it was going to run her down. In a flat sprint, in track shoes, she probably could have won a forty-yard dash – likewise on a semi-maintained dirt road. But going barefoot on this rough tundra left her limping like a wounded deer.

She was, however, still a gymnast – one of those things she'd learned young.

As the dragon closed, Anna cut hard right, aiming for the nearest tree, and leaped for the lowest overhanging branch.

She actually felt the teeth catch the paper-thin fabric of her hospital smock as she swung her legs up over her head. The jerk nearly pulled her loose from the branch, but the teeth cut the frail fabric and tore away.

It probably could have gotten her anyway as her legs swung back down and she hung for a moment, helpless – fortunately, the dragon thought the fabric *was* her, and it pulled away, tearing at the mouthful like a bulldog. Then it realized its mistake, spitting out white tufts, and turned back, just as Anna swung her legs back up onto the branch.

This time it was her hair, already shorn by dragon teeth, nearly snagged by the beast's lunging bite.

Anna settled up on the branch like a crossbar, looking down. She rose to her haunches, her skin scuffed and bleeding from the rough bark.

Sheena, Queen of the Jungle, she thought balefully.

The dragon pawed at the bottom of the tree, looking up.

Komodo monitors in nature spent the majority of their infancy in trees, hiding from the cannibalistic adults, who were too heavy for the thin upper branches.

It didn't mean the big ones couldn't still climb, though.

Anna craned her head to the treetop, knowing she was a good deal heavier than a baby dragon.

She began to climb.

Below her, the dragon's claws latched into the bark and the three-meter lizard scaled the main trunk like a skink.

Anna picked the heaviest branch she could find and climbed out to the end, clinging to the surrounding limbs for balance and support.

When she looked back, the dragon was already *there* – peering at her from behind the trunk, the tongue actually *licking* its lips.

With the agility of a squirrel, it circled its bulk around the tree until it stepped onto her branch, testing the weight with one claw.

The branch creaked and the dragon paused.

It couldn't follow her out, Anna told herself.

It was fat, this dragon was. And heavy.

The creature's massive bulk recalled a fun fact about dragon gluttony from her night with Taylor, when Anna had learned more about Komodo monitors than she'd ever wanted – she knew they were ravenous, and that a hundred-and-seventy-five-pound dragon might eat a hundred-and-forty-pounds in a single meal.

That was ALL of her – the best parts first, of course, but there would be nothing left.

They were not, Anna realized, at a stand-off on the branch.

The dragon took another step and the limb creaked even more alarmingly.

For a moment, the dragon seemed to stare almost smugly, giving her a moment to figure it out. Then it stepped out again, eliciting another loud crack.

It would snap the branch, Anna realized. It was going to drop her to the forest floor.

Anna gauged the distance to the ground – she had already taken one bad fall tonight – she was looking at at least a twenty-foot drop.

The dragon's tongue lolled, and it took another step. The creak grew louder.

Anna held fast to the surrounding branches, trying to take her weight.

But now the dragon was only a few feet away.

If she let go, the branch beneath her would give.

But she was in range of the teeth.

The tongue reached out one more time, savoring the taste.

Then the teeth lunged forward.

Anna screamed, helpless and trapped – she actually *saw* past the rows of teeth down into the pale-pink gullet as the lizard went for her face.

Then, as if answering her scream, a shot rang out.

The dragon's head splatted, as its brains blew out one side.

Anna actually felt the wind as the snap of teeth fell short, followed by the spray of blood and brain-matter.

The giant-lizard fell limp.

With a final crack, the branch broke away under the beast's dead weight.

Anna screamed again, as she clung to the surrounding limbs.

The dragon corpse tumbled, dropping heavily and bonelessly, cleaving branches all the way down, flipping over to hit the ground on its back.

Another shot rang out, apparently just to make sure, and the dragon's head kicked again. The massive body continued to twist as if in pain.

Anna saw the lights of the Jeep shining into the grove, Burroughs behind the wheel. Colin was standing outside the passenger door, his rifle aimed across the hood.

Once upon a time, he had made her feel safe. She had pined for ten years about how safe he had made her feel.

Now as his shadow came from behind the Jeep, a dark indistinct shape moving towards her tree, her heart was touched by a cold fright she'd not felt even out on the ocean.

The dragon continued to stubbornly squirm in lingering death spasms.

Colin fired one more bullet into the twisting corpse, if nothing else to drive the point home – the dragon was NOT the top predator on *this* island.

Then he turned and looked up into the branches.

"Anna? I see you. Come on down."

And then, with the first sternness of impatience, "Don't make me come up there and get you."

The point became moot, however, as the branches she clung to broke away, sending her tumbling to the forest floor.

CHAPTER 36

Anna hit every branch on the way down, battering her already beaten body like a gauntlet of gnarled, wooden clubs, depositing her in a bruised and bloody heap, nearly on top of the dead dragon.

The beast had been shot twice in the head and once in the chest, yet it still writhed. The top of the skull was blown apart, but the greedy predator-gleam in its eyes never changed. And the mouth still gaped, as if it might snap shut on her like a mousetrap. The dead claws flexed and grabbed.

Anna scrambled away, shuddering. Then she heard several more shots fire, nearly over her shoulder.

More dragons were encroaching, and Colin shot three in rapid succession. The big lizards kicked and thrashed in the dirt – which bothered the others not a whit.

Monitors were already active in the early morning hours, and these dragons had been roused by the scent of blood.

They had also obviously been following the big one like a pack leader, ceding territory just at safe range. Now that the king-lizard was gone, Anna guessed every two-bit pretender was going to be jockeying for the throne.

She heard Burroughs calling from the Jeep.

"I told you, the smell of blood only stimulates them."

"Right," Colin said, shouldering his rifle and continuing to shoot several more.

And while the dragons remained curiously immune to fear, the ruse was now working in practice by providing fresh blood and dead meat right there among the middle of them, halting their inexorable march, as the opportunistic lizards fell upon their still-kicking companions, unabashedly cannibalizing the fresh corpses.

But there were more of them, skulking through the rustling grass on all sides, popping up out of the brush, scenting the air.

"We'd best not tarry," Burroughs said mildly.

Colin turned to Anna. She looked up at him, her eyes wide as a cat's.

"Come on now," Colin said, extending his hand.

"I'm not going anywhere with you," Anna said, crawling back. "Are you crazy?"

"I'm not leaving you out here," Colin replied. "Whatever you may think of me now, I still care about you, and I'll drag you back with me if I have to."

He took a step forward.

"Once you're safe, we can talk about what happens next."

"What's to talk about? How I feel about my husband's murder? Or my best friend?"

Colin frowned.

"First things first." He reached for her.

Anna scrambled back, kicking, trying to fight, but then she felt his hands on her, and he was every bit as strong as she knew he would be. She was utterly, laughably, helpless. He pulled her to her feet like her father had pulled her out her sandbox when she was seven. He cinched his grip on one arm and the scruff of her neck, brooking no resistance.

Colin sighed regretfully, turning back to the Jeep. "Mr. Burroughs? Would you please take us back...?"

That was all he got out as he realized Burroughs was already there, suddenly right behind them.

Colin stiffened, letting out a startled grunt.

Sidling up in cold-blooded silence, Burroughs had slipped a thin silver blade like a stiletto into his liver.

Colin's face froze in a stark rictus of agony.

Burroughs twisted the blade with the professional expertise of a surgeon.

Colin staggered, and Anna felt him release her, throwing her to the ground, as he turned to defend himself.

But the damage was already done. His legs folded underneath him and he stumbled.

Unhurried, Burroughs bent to retrieve his pistol from Colin's belt, taking a calm moment to check the safety, the ammo, and the muzzle.

Then he leveled the gun and shot Colin in the stomach.

Colin let out another horse-kicked grunt, and doubled over to the ground.

Burroughs watched him twist and kick his last few seconds away – at the end, no different than the lizard after all.

Anna knew Burroughs could have shot him in the heart. Or the head.

But he wanted something that would *hurt*.

Colin finally stiffened and lay still.

Burroughs shook his head, tiredly, in the manner of dealing with a tiresome chore.

Anna blinked up from the ground, speechless.

Burroughs kicked Colin's motionless form, experimentally, glancing warily at the perimeter, where loitering dragons perked with ever-greater interest at the smell of every mounting corpse.

The old man smiled to the dragons.

"Pickings are good tonight, aren't they?"

Then he turned back to Anna.

He raised the gun.

"I'm sorry, Mrs. Miller," he said.

Then, over the idling Jeep, Anna heard a second motor, that suddenly revved hard and loud.

Burroughs paused, looking over his shoulder as one of his own four-wheelers suddenly burst into the clearing, squirreling sideways from the rocky precipice that impersonated a road.

The four-wheeler actually seemed to coil, as it lurched forward, charging Burroughs like a bull after a flag.

"*Taylor*," Burroughs cursed. He raised his pistol and began to shoot.

At least two shots hit their target. Anna saw Taylor jerk in the driver's seat, and the four-wheeler swerved wildly.

But Taylor yanked the rig back on-course.

The revving engine was an animal's growl as Burroughs was now forced to turn and run.

He was not quite fast enough – the wheel clipped him as he leaped aside, and he was sent rolling, before the four-wheeler itself spun out of control, flipped and crashed.

Taylor threw himself clear, letting the rig tumble into wreckage.

For a heartbeat, the shaggy caveman lay stunned on the ground, before staggering to his feet, shaking off the impact like a wounded animal.

Now he pulled a canister from his pack and pulled the pin. Anna smelled the acid stench of tear-gas.

Just as Burroughs was clambering to his feet, Taylor pitched it at him.

There was a simultaneous gunshot, combined with a fusillade of profanity as Burroughs clawed his eyes.

Then Anna felt herself grabbed and yanked to her feet. Taylor's grip was tight as a vice.

"Come on," he whispered tersely, and Anna realized for the first time how badly he had been shot. The pistol had hit his arm and shoulder – bleeding quite badly, thank you – but now she saw his duct-taped abdomen – and the blood seeping through like a running faucet.

He left a path like red paint, splattered on the leaves, as he dragged her along behind.

Back in the clearing, the tear-gas had scattered the dragons, but Burroughs was on his feet, one hand over his face, wiping his tearing eyes. Half-blind, he emptied his pistol into the brush. Anna heard bullets zinging past.

"I told you he was crazy," Taylor said, pulling them both low. "No one ever listens."

His grip remained locked like handcuffs around her wrist.

Anna felt the wetness of blood on his hand, as he led her deeper into the bush.

CHAPTER 37

Taylor led her through the dark as if by braille. Not quite able to stretch into a full run, he moved in a hurried, ape-like lurch. Anna could clearly see where he had taped-over a hole the size of a silver-dollar blown out his back.

They broke through the foliage onto an open plateau. At some point in the past, lava had pooled in this particular peak, recently enough that sediment hadn't yet accumulated sufficient topsoil for plant growth. The flat lava plates did, however, trap several large pools of rainwater. Taylor stopped at one of these, wincing as he splashed his shoulder and back.

Anna bent to look at his wounds.

"These... this is bad," she said.

"I noticed that," Taylor said. "Think it's going to kill me?"

Anna didn't answer. But, yes, she thought so.

After that, how long would she last alone?

She felt a clammy finger of dread at the thought of dying out here – of being left as nothing but carrion.

The dragons would sniff you out, dismember you, and swallow the pieces whole. It happened to every dead thing on the island.

Might it not just be better to walk right back out into the ocean? Right back the way they came? Drowning was preferable to being devoured.

Of course, there were sharks. It was like Lost World Alcatraz.

"We need to get back to the compound," Anna said. "We can call for help."

Taylor chuckled lightly, shaking his head. "I've got a couple of hours left," he said.

"There's the infirmary," Anna said.

"Yeah, about that," Taylor said. "Before I came after you, I lit the place on fire. Kind of a nihilistic impulse, I admit. Poetic justice. Burn it all down. Fire purifies."

He sighed. "So. Sorry about that. I guess I kind of had the idea of making my last few hours count."

On that note, he turned a thoughtful eye to Anna.

"So," he said, "wanna make-out?"

Anna eyed him warily. Three times he'd made a variation of that joke.

Ironically, she almost responded reflexively with her long-standing, by-rote, *I'm married*-line, before she realized she wasn't anymore – she was widowed.

So instead she just glared.

"No?" Taylor shrugged. "Oh well. Just as well. The last blond I met got me in trouble."

"Lorena Burroughs," Anna said.

Taylor nodded. "I know. Another man's wife. I don't deny the sin. I just thought the penance was overkill."

"As sins go," Anna said, "adultery is one of the big ones. It's been known to start wars."

Taylor choked a quip of laughter, and Anna saw blood on his lips as he did so.

"No doubt there," he said.

He spit blood.

"I'm not saying it was a set-up. But we had *never* been alone before – not *once*. And just suddenly he was *there*. The *second* we touched."

Taylor shut his eyes for a moment. One sweet snapshot in a gallery of horrors.

"It *was* a good kiss."

He shrugged.

"Still, that's a pretty strict interpretation of adultery. That's some no-shit Old Testament Wrath."

His eyes narrowed.

"But I'm guessing," he said, "that's not the story *he* told."

Anna shook her head.

"You attacked her on the veranda," she said. "She fell over the edge."

"Mmmm hmmm," Taylor mused. "And did he explain how I managed to end up on the run like a hunted animal?"

"He said you jumped after her. You escaped into the woods."

"Well," he said, "that part's right. But it wasn't from the veranda."

He shook his head. "Come on. That's a fifty-foot drop."

"What's your version?"

Taylor glanced reflexively over his shoulder. There was, as yet, no sound of pursuit, but Taylor was looking back where it had happened.

He pulled his tattered rag of a shirt past the two fresh bullet holes to reveal an older scar, long-healed.

"That's where he shot me with a tranq-dart," he said, "when he walked up on us at the veranda. I woke up in handcuffs, down on the feeding docks."

Anna shuddered. She remembered that balcony.

"He wanted me to watch," Taylor said, "while he threw her in with the lizards."

Taylor shut his eyes. "I... heard her scream."

His voice drifted.

"We were never alone before," he repeated, shaking his head as if to deny the injustice of it. "I was always careful. I mean, she was the boss' trophy wife.

"*And,*" he continued, "I'd never got it in so many words, but I was under the impression that, during her time on the island, there had been other caretakers before me. Mine was not the first head to be turned. The lesson was she had learned not to act overly familiar.

"That," he said, "is something I've wondered a lot about since."

Taylor fell silent, hunting for the proper words to justify his existence – or at least not condemn it.

He came up with a shrug.

"What can I say? Any man who saw her would have had thoughts about her. We saw each other every day. We lived on a tropical island. It was just... a moment of chemistry."

Chemistry, Anna thought – a physical reaction.

A lizard had chemistry.

That had been what she'd shared with Colin. Somehow, right now that felt dirtier to her, even than some actual physical affair. Whether she'd admitted it or not, when she'd said 'no' to Colin that night, she'd spent the next ten years comparing him to Marcus – always to Marcus' detriment.

And *oh*, how Marcus had tried to live up to her fantasy.

God, she felt so ashamed.

That was a look she saw mirrored in Taylor's haunted eyes – old wounds hemorrhaging inside – somewhere near the heart.

"We all get tested, I suppose," he said. "It was a small indiscretion, but an indiscretion nonetheless. I mean, who knows what might have happened if he hadn't walked up on us."

The sweet snapshot of memory turned abruptly sour – a whiff of Hot Kitty before *conditioning*.

Anna swallowed dryly. "What happened? After he threw her over?"

"I... just went after her." He threw up his hands helplessly. "Stupid. I knew it was already over."

His eyes narrowed dangerously. "If I'd just gone after *him* instead..."

Taylor made momentary clawing gestures with his bloody hands.

But then the spark of rage subsided. He was just too damn tired.

"I guess it wasn't until just that second that I realized..."

He stopped, letting it remain unsaid. No matter how he told it, he still came off badly.

"I just jumped. I think I knocked Burroughs on his ass on the way, but..." He shrugged. "I just flat frog-leaped and rolled. Damn near broke my leg."

He shook his head.

"It didn't matter. The dragons... they already... one of them had torn out her throat – a *big* one. The others... they were tearing at her face."

Anna shut her eyes. She didn't have to imagine. She'd seen it up close.

And, of course, Lorena had *her* face.

She wondered if it had been that big dragon on the fence – and perhaps that was why it seemed so fearless of Hot Kitty?

Maybe *that* dragon knew Hot Kitty meant food.

"Burroughs started shooting," Taylor said, "and I just ran. I jumped the gate. I was stuck in those goddamned handcuffs for a week."

He fell silent, seeing it all again, and this time when he spoke, his voice cracked.

"I just can't get over the fact that *happened* to her. I couldn't stop it. And it was because of *me*."

He nodded to himself as he spoke – the rocking monkey.

"Yeah," he said, softly. "Still having a hard time with that."

Anna reached out slowly to touch his shoulder, and still the rocking. Taylor froze feral at her touch.

But then he relaxed and clasped her hand – not *gripped* like before.

"You know," he said, "it's not like I had any illusions about her. I mean, she answered an *ad*, for God's sake. But you learn not to judge people over the things they do for shelter. I answered an ad to get here too."

Taylor wiped a blood-smeared hand across tearing eyes.

"Hell, I'm not even sure if she was his first mail-order bride. I don't know how many people he's fed to his goddamned lizards. I know there was never any more live-on staff after that day. And I've been watching for five years."

He looked down at his duct-taped, but still-leaking gut.

"But I guess he finally got me," he said.

At that moment, not far distant, they heard the sound of the approaching Jeep.

CHAPTER 38

Taylor stood, groaning painfully, looking east.

"He's moving along the coast. Probably less than half-a-mile out."

He turned a resigned eye at Anna. "I suppose you told him where to find the cave?"

Anna said nothing – answer enough.

"We've got to keep moving." He held up his wet, red-stained hand to the breeze. "The dragons are smelling me. We've got to stay ahead of the wind."

He hiked his pack, ready to pull her along, if necessary.

"Do we even have a plan?" Anna asked hopelessly.

Taylor shrugged.

"Just going to keep running until you die?"

Taylor quipped a brief laugh. "Don't we all?"

He started to reach towards her, but Anna stood, acquiescing voluntarily.

The flat plateau was hedged by trees, but like the main compound, there was a strip cut through the foliage, joining the coast.

"Burroughs is going to have some idea where we are. He knows the geography. We used to use these flats for helicopter drops." Taylor pointed to the cropped road, cleared along a fault-line, split in the volcanic rock, providing a natural gap in the trees.

"But," he said, "if we can beat him to the coast..."

Anna, however, had doubts. Taylor was wobbling on his feet. Secondly, the sound of the Jeep engine, to her ear, lay directly in their path.

And the first two might not matter, because even as he led her into the dark hollow between the trees, they could already hear the bushes around them rustling. Taylor stopped, hunting for movement in the dark.

As Anna's eyes adjusted, she realized there were already several dragons ahead of them, blocking the path.

In the fresh absence of their recently fallen king, the largest of them seemed to deliberately strut and posture, ready to tear into each other as readily as the potential mammalian prey.

Stimulated and aggressive – hungry, predatory, *and* pugnacious.

Taylor stopped, facing them off. Anna felt his blood-wet hand on her shoulder, reflexively shielding her like a kid in a car-seat.

He pulled his pack, taking quick stock of his cache of weapons.

Several squirt bottles – bleach, gasoline – a couple of road flares. And of course, a tin of Hot Kitty.

Anna made a silent promise to herself that, if she lived, she would never wear Hot Kitty ever again. If she smelled it in a department store, she would break the bottle on the shelf.

Taylor also had one more tin of tear-gas. He pulled the cap and tossed the tin down the path.

The visible dragons scattered. There was similar – and uncomfortably widespread – rustling in the surrounding brush. In the darkness, the dorsal-fin tales were invisible.

But they were out there. And it was a lot.

After a few minutes, the gas began to disperse. Taylor grabbed Anna's hand.

"Okay," he said, "we've got to move quickly."

That, however, was when a gunshot rang out.

Taylor jerked, barking out a heavy grunt of pain, before throwing himself to the ground, dragging Anna down with him. Blood spurted from the middle of his thigh. The bullet had passed directly through the femur.

There would be no more walking tonight.

Anna knelt beside him.

Taylor took stock of his injuries.

Enough. It was enough.

"Damn," he whispered.

About a hundred yards away, the front headlights of the Jeep switched on, spotlighting them in its high-beams.

No doubt Burroughs was standing just behind those blinding lights. He had probably scoped them out with some kind of fancy infra-red lens.

He'd centered the shot on Taylor's leg. Apparently, he didn't want to kill him just yet. Or more likely, not that fast.

He wanted something that would *hurt*.

Anna heard a car door slam, the engine revved, and the headlights began to bounce in their direction.

Taylor lay in Anna's arms, watching impassively – the rabbit finally run down.

For a moment, Anna thought the headlights were simply going to drive over the top of them, but they stopped ten feet short.

The door opened and Burroughs stepped out. He was holding the pistol he'd used to murder Colin.

In unhurried ritual, he checked his safety and his ammo, as he strolled in leisurely fashion, until he stood directly over them, a dark shadow framed in blinding light, ready to pass judgment.

"Well," Taylor said, looking up.

"Well," Burroughs responded, looking down.

Anna blinked back and forth between the two of them.

"You've led me a merry chase, Mr. Taylor," Burroughs said. "I must admit, the things I once admired about you are still true. You're a tenacious bastard."

The old man shook his head wonderingly. "Do you know the lengths I went to make *sure* you were dead? I took samples of your blood we kept in storage, and mixed it with their food. I ransacked your room for every personal item and tossed it to them as chew toys, anything with your scent or DNA. The fact that you've survived this long, is really a testament to Darwin."

The old man stroked his chin thoughtfully. "You know, it was recently suggested to me that these animals have reached their evolutionary end. Perhaps you are evidence that this is true. Five long years, and an entire island of prehistoric monsters couldn't catch you.

"No," Burroughs said. "It took another human being."

He smiled, nodding to Anna.

"Perhaps even a woman," he said. "Beauty is always the foil."

Taylor eyed him directly.

"Always," he agreed.

"You know, Mr. Taylor," Burroughs said, "I believe up until just now, I've been operating under a delusion." He waved generally to the surrounding forests. "This primeval world. I thought its purity somehow made it better.

"And the dragons," he said, "because they were primitive and efficient, I judged them better able to survive."

Burroughs shook his head. "I now believe it is really quite the opposite. They are dated and obsolete – just as I have allowed myself to be, hiding away from the world on this island. A fascination built on an inferiority complex, I suppose."

The old man smiled – the smile of a very old lizard.

"I think you've cured me," he said.

He raised the pistol. "I'm a frumpy, doddering old man. But I got *you*."

Burroughs pulled the trigger, firing a bullet with medical precision into Taylor's stomach.

Anna screamed as Taylor bucked in her arms, gasping and spitting blood.

She felt his hands grip her tightly, and for a split second pulled her close.

Their eyes locked – Anna wondered who he was seeing – but he choked out two words.

"I'm... sorry."

She felt him stiffen and clench.

Then he relaxed and lay still.

Anna let him go. She felt the helpless sting of tears.

Burroughs' smile was grim and satisfied – his voice was the purr of an old lion.

"I've been waiting a long time for that," he said. "*Too* long."

He turned to Anna. "I suppose I have you to thank."

Anna blinked through tears as the pistol now swiveled in her direction.

"*Why?*" Anna asked.

And Burroughs stopped.

CHAPTER 39

"You never know about people," Burroughs said, "until you see them tested."

He shrugged – *ergo*. "They were tested."

"You murdered your wife," Anna said.

Burroughs frowned.

"It really was a sordid business," he said, eyeing Anna knowingly. "Rather like that with Captain Braddock and your late husband."

Anna shut her eyes.

But I didn't *do* anything, she thought. But she knew that would carry no coin in this court, and might even serve to condemn. We may sin in word, thought, or deed.

Besides, it really wasn't about that.

"I was waiting to find out what Taylor told you," Burroughs said. "It's really too bad. Otherwise, you all would have been rescued by now. Left to play out whatever turns your own scandalous little lives might have taken."

"Unfortunately," he said, "there are skeletons in my own closet that I would not have see the light of day."

"So," Burroughs said, sadly, "at this point, it would be better for all of you to have been simply lost at sea. Even if wreckage from your boat is found, there would be no reason to look at this island out of all the others.

"And *really*," he said, shaking his head, "the *lot* of you. The world will be no poorer."

He raised the gun again.

The purposeful look in his eyes finally broke her.

Helpless and frustrated, she began to weep.

"*Please...*" She held up her hands, covering her face.

Burroughs shook his head regretfully.

"I could just let you go," he said, waving at the surrounding forest. "But wouldn't that just be a cruelty? I doubt you have the survival skills Mr. Taylor had. The dragons would make short work of you. Best to just put you down quick."

Anna had started to crawl away, and Burroughs stepped to follow, before she gained room to coil and run.

"*No...*," she moaned as she tried to scramble back, but Burroughs grabbed her roughly, with every bit of Colin's strength, pulling her up to her knees.

He pulled the hammer back on the pistol and placed the gun to her head. He probably really *did* look at it like a kindness – it wasn't something that would *hurt*.

"Not that it matters," he said, "but I *am* sorry, Mrs. Miller. Really, though, what are my choices? Trust you to go back to the world and not say anything forever?"

Anna didn't bother to protest.

"The other option," Burroughs said, "would be to keep you here."

The hand on the scuff of her neck turned her face-up so he could see her.

She did look like his wife, after all.

"What do you think, Mrs. Miller? You're widowed now. Suppose I decide to keep you on as the new trophy-wife?"

Now he actually smiled a little, considering.

But then shook his head sadly.

"Except, that would be a bondage, wouldn't it? Not like Lorena, who entered here freely and of her own will. It would also put *me* in the uncomfortable position of knowing every moment that the key to your freedom would be my not being here anymore."

He was playing her, she realized. Making her bargain with herself. Giving her an out, only to yank it away.

That was when she knew he was enjoying this, and any regret was crocodile-tears.

He was reptilian, Lorena Burroughs had said – not capable of empathy.

His needs were more basic. The mind was just there to rationalize.

"So you see?" he said. "I have no choice. This is just self-defense."

Locked in Burroughs' grip, the sheer, self-serving sanctimony sparked a moment of pure rage, and Anna suddenly lashed out, clawing at the hand holding her, trying to bite.

"*Liar!*" she barked, angry tears choking her words.

Burroughs tightened his grip, quelling the rebellion with one smart shake. He looked down on her with angry, dangerous eyes.

Then he threw her hard to the ground. She hit the rocks painfully and lay stunned.

Burroughs stood over her.

"You're right," he said.

His face wasn't angry now. Or even faux-sympathetic.

Anna realized she had been wrong in the infirmary – he hadn't been looking for absolution.

He was just dying to *talk* about it.

"You remember the boy who died?" Burroughs said. "The one who fell among the dragons? Well, I told you the truth before – I truly *didn't* remember the incident. At the time."

"But then," he said, "one day, I did."

A ghost of a smile touched his lips, small and secret.

"And what I remembered was that I pushed him."

Burroughs shook his head in wonder.

"Isn't the unconscious mind fascinating? The impulse to *do* something like that, almost simultaneous with the action wiped from my consciousness. A psychological defense mechanism? I know I could have passed a lie-detector test."

Anna shut her eyes – Burroughs had been four years old.

For a moment, the gun wavered, as the old man reflected fondly on a long-ago past. He sighed deeply, as if with the satisfied puff of a pipe.

"Have you ever had an alcoholic black-out? Where your memories suddenly flashback? That's exactly what it was like. And once it came back, I remembered everything."

Burroughs breathed another long drag.

"The boy was a bully. And no one would *do* anything about it. So *I* did.

"And it was *easy*," he said. "Just like throwing a grasshopper in a spider's web. After that, I wasn't afraid of anyone anymore. I knew what I could do to them."

Anna wondered how many times *that* came up over the years.

Burroughs smiled, reading her thoughts.

"Pretty much anyone you're around long enough will give you a reason to kill them, don't you think? I mean, how many times have you said you'd kill your husband?"

Anna shook her head. "That's not the same..."

"I know, I know," he interrupted impatiently. "Figuratively versus literally. But imagine if every time you said it, you were all alone, with easy opportunity, and no consequences."

He stood above her.

"Take away consequences, that frees you up a lot."

Now Burroughs brought the gun up and aimed it at her head.

Pretense was gone now. His eyes were merciless.

A total lack of empathy.

Anna saw his finger start to squeeze the trigger.

She actually *heard* the retort of the gunshot.

Above her, Burroughs' face seemed to explode – the top of his skull, down to the middle of his forehead, blew out just above the eyes.

Anna blinked as she was splattered in his blood.

Burroughs fell forward, as if leaping bodily on top of her. Anna shrieked under his weight as he flopped like loose meat and lay still.

"Tell you what," a choking voice said, "*there's* your fucking consequences."

A cough.

"You son of a bitch."

Taylor was hanging on the door to the Jeep, Burroughs' own rifle over one shoulder.

Now he collapsed to the flat-volcanic rock.

Anna pushed the corpse of Richard Burroughs off of her, rising to her feet.

"Taylor?"

She knelt by his side. He looked up at her, and for the first time since she'd known him, he looked frightened.

"I don't want to be eaten," he said, and she felt him tense with age-old primitive dread. He glanced around the clearing.

No dragons yet. The tear-gas was still keeping them off. It was also possible they were simply waiting until all the human ruckus resolved itself, and then just freeload off the kill.

But they were always there. And never far.

"You'll take care of it, right?" Taylor said. He grabbed her hand, and she felt none of his ape-like strength from before.

Anna nodded. "I promise."

His grip relaxed, but did not let go.

Anna let him cling to her. It was the least she could do. As cavemen went, this guy had been pretty decent to her.

"I'll tell people," Anna said. "I'll make sure people know who Richard Burroughs was."

And then suddenly, he cinched his grip, his face tense and dramatic.

"*No*," he said, in a gravelly voice, "I AM Richard Burroughs."

And then, deadpan, over her aghast expression, the imitation of mechanical breathing.

"What?" he said. "No laugh?"

He shook his head, coughing. "I swear, I just don't know what's *funny* anymore."

Anna actually chirped a quip of exasperated laughter and swatted him lightly on the cheek.

He choked a little and smiled.

And then, just like that, with that last spark of jovial camaraderie, she felt him leave her, like the rustle of a wind. And then she was alone.

She blinked, aware of the difference. Forever and a few seconds ago, he had been there with her. Everything else from now on would be *after*.

Anna sat there for a while.

The stillness, however, was an illusion.

Now that the ruckus had died down and the residue of the tear-gas faded, the dragons would be on the move.

Anna spent a few minutes pulling Taylor into the back of the Jeep. His limp weight was like dragging a two-hundred-pound bag of sand.

As she fished the keys from Burroughs' pocket, she caught the old man's eyes staring from beneath his shattered skull – just like the dragon's that had chased her up the tree – and the expression on both their dead faces was the same – utterly unaltered from what they were in life.

She left Burroughs' body behind.   As she started the Jeep, she saw the first of the dragons encroaching at the edge of the clearing.

Anna didn't hang around to watch.   Instead, she drove along the precarious coast, back up to the makeshift road that led back to the house.

When she arrived, she did indeed find the place ablaze.

The steel, glass, and ornamental marble that provided the structure of the building, of course, did not burn, but Taylor had certainly done his job from within – the interior glowed in an almost solid torch.

She didn't know it, but she thought the same thing Taylor did – the windows looked like the eyes and teeth of a giant jack o-lantern.

Cut, of course, into the fangs of a dragon.

Anna parked across from the footbridge, which she saw had been left deliberately open – as had the garage across from the pit.

The pit itself was largely evacuated, the lizards evidently having taken over the fence for the forest, once the blaze got started in the building above.

Except for that one big bastard on the fence, who still sat sentry, watching the castle burn.

Still standing guard.

CHAPTER 40

Anna stretched out on the pool-deck, on a lawn-chair in the sun, a glass of wine in her hand, much as had Lorena Burroughs up to the very last day of her life.

The view was spectacular, overlooking the ocean.

All to herself.

Well, almost. Every now and again, she would hear one of her barricades being knocked over. But she was learning to deal with that.

The interior of the place had burned out – one consequence, of which, was that it left her wine warm, while she preferred chilled.

Another was that all the electrical mechanisms for the garage door Taylor had left open no longer worked, so the dragons wandered freely, in and out.

They had also broken down the doors that led up the stairway to the main lobby, forcing her to block that avenue with whatever refuse she could find – including the heavy, fossilized bones of the Megalania – which had survived the fire, but now that the place was hers, Anna had decided she didn't like very much.

It was actually the smaller dragons that were the most trouble. Without a sealed door, they just crawled through a physical barricade.

She was mostly okay in her room at night, with its locking door, but she had to watch her step in the hall.

All in all, it was a sight better than a cave on the edge of a cliff. Anna was learning to count her blessings.

She did what Taylor had taught her. Whenever one of them got a little too curious, she poked it with a stick.

For emergencies, she had a few shots left in the pistol Burroughs had used to kill Colin, and another couple in the rifle Taylor had used to kill *him*. There were also, theoretically, more weapons in Burroughs' gun cabinet, if she could just figure out how to open the damn thing.

Of course, she still kept a bottle of bleach handy. It was, after all, something that would *hurt* – and she was already coming to understand how quickly you could come to hate them.

And despite her vow, she was heavily endowed with Hot Kitty – in lieu of a hot bath for the foreseeable future.

She had kept her promise to Taylor. With appreciable effort, she managed to wrestle his body to the roof, up to one of those goth towers that doubled as a chopper-dock – and she set him up his own funeral pyre – a dolly from the infirmary, lashed in place, doused in a bottle of gasoline from Taylor's own pack.

Anna lit the fire, and she had kept it burning from dawn every morning since, adding branches and dry leaves, sending a plume of smoke high into the air, hopefully to serve as an SOS that might finally get her rescued.

She thought Taylor would have liked that. Practical *and* symbolic.

How different might it have been, she wondered, without these walls? The base structure remained – there were a number of surviving bedrooms, as well as the sealed storage lockers. She had food, supplies. Hell, she had a deck and a pool – stagnate and green, and full of skittering bugs, but a pool nonetheless.

Burroughs had also said he had a cleaning and maintenance crew out once a month. In theory, all she had to do was wait until they showed up.

Of course, Anna didn't know if it was a pre-scheduled visit, or if they waited on his call. How inclined might they be to simply blow-off this out-of-the-way stop, if they didn't hear from him for a month or two? Or six?

She would have to wait and see. And stay alive until then.

The pit below remained mostly vacant – a thorough spray-down with tear-gas, along with *not* feeding them, had gone a long way towards clearing out the dragons.

Except for that one big bastard still sitting on the fence.

Never flitting, still is sitting, STILL is sitting...

It just waited, as if it knew there would be no one to burn a pyre for *her*.

The dragon was looking in her direction – it always did, its tongue lolling out, tasting her on the air.

And its eyes have all the seeming of a demon's that is dreaming...

Lurid lyric. Penned by a madman.

Anna shuddered.

To chase away the chill, she refilled her glass of wine.

She shut her eyes. stretching out on her chair in the sun, just like any dream-vacation, in a bikini by the pool – the blue water grown fetid and green, with her eyes ever-wary at the corners, and her ears perked like a hunted deer.

She had every reason for optimism. The smoke sent out a clear, obvious sign that should be visible for miles. There *should* still be a search crew looking for The Challenger. It had only been a few days, and the weather had been good.

Someone *should* come along, sooner than later.

In the meantime, she had a finite supply of food and bottled water – and even access to the fresh rainwater that fed the falls.

She was set-up well. And she wasn't worried. She hadn't even bothered to take full stock of what Burroughs had supplied in the pantry.

Of course, one reason she hadn't, was because to do so, would be to draw up an estimate on the length of her potential life.

One month or six months could make a big difference either way.

But she wasn't quite ready to think about all that just yet.

Either someone would come before she ran out of supplies or the dragons would get her.

Anna herself would have very little to say about it.

So she sipped her warm wine, and tipped a toast to the dragon that watched her on the fence.

Together they waited to see which came first.

THE END

SEVERED**PRESS**

 facebook.com/severedpress
 twitter.com/severedpress

CHECK OUT OTHER GREAT DINOSAUR BOOKS

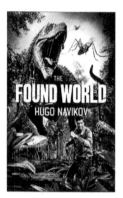

THE FOUND WORLD
by **Hugo Navikov**

A powerful global cabal wants adventurer Brett Russell to retrieve a superweapon stolen by the scientist who built it. To entice him to travel underneath one of the most dangerous volcanoes on Earth to find the scientist, this shadowy organization will pay him the only thing he cares about: information that will allow him to avenge his family's murder.

But before he can get paid, he and his team must enter an underground hellscape of killer plants, giant insects, terrifying dinosaurs, and an army of other predators never previously seen by man.

At the end of this journey awaits a revelation that could alter the fate of mankind ... if they can make it back from this horrifying found world.

HOUSE OF THE GODS
by **Davide Mana**

High above the steamy jungle of the Amazon basin, rise the flat plateaus known as the Tepui, the House of the Gods. Lost worlds of unknown beauty, a naturalistic wonder, each an ecology onto itself, shunned by the local tribes for centuries. The House of the Gods was not made for men.

But now, the crew and passengers of a small charter plane are about to find what was hidden for sixty million years.

Lost on an island in the clouds 10,000 feet above the jungle, surrounded by dinosaurs, hunted by mysterious mercenaries, the survivors of Sligo Air flight 001 will quickly learn the only rule of life on Earth: Extinction.

CHECK OUT OTHER GREAT DINOSAUR BOOKS

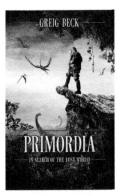

PRIMORDIA
by **Greig Beck**

Ben Cartwright, former soldier, home to mourn the loss of his father stumbles upon cryptic letters from the past between the author, Arthur Conan Doyle and his great, great grandfather who vanished while exploring the Amazon jungle in 1908.

Amazingly, these letters lead Ben to believe that his ancestor's expedition was the basis for Doyle's fantastical tale of a lost world inhabited by long extinct creatures. As Ben digs some more he finds clues to the whereabouts of a lost notebook that might contain a map to a place that is home to creatures that would rewrite everything known about history, biology and evolution.

But other parties now know about the notebook, and will do anything to obtain it. For Ben and his friends, it becomes a race against time and against ruthless rivals.

In the remotest corners of Venezuela, along winding river trails known only to lost tribes, and through near impenetrable jungle, Ben and his novice team find a forbidden place more terrifying and dangerous than anything they could ever have imagined.

PANGAEA EXILES
by **Jeff Brackett**

Tried and convicted for his crimes, Sean Barrow is sent into temporal exile—banished to a time so far before recorded history that there is no chance that he, or any other criminal sent back, has any chance of altering history.

Now Sean must find a way to survive more than 200 million years in the past, in a world populated by monstrous creatures that would rend him limb from limb if they got the chance. And that's just his fellow prisoners.

The dinosaurs are almost as bad.

CHECK OUT OTHER GREAT DINOSAUR BOOKS

FLIPSIDE
by JAKE BIBLE

The year is 2046 and dinosaurs are real.

Time bubbles across the world, many as large as one hundred square miles, turn like clockwork, revealing prehistoric landscapes from the Cretaceous Period.

They reveal the Flipside.

Now, thirty years after the first Turn, the clockwork is breaking down as one of the world's powers has decided to exploit the phenomenon for their own gain, possibly destroying everything then and now in the process.

A MAN OUT OF TIME
by Christopher Laflan

Five years after the Chinese Axis detonated an unknown weapon of mass destruction off the southern coast of the United States, Special Ops Sergeant John Crider and the members of Shadow Company have finally captured what they all hope will lead to the end of the war. Unfortunately, the population within the United States is no longer sustainable. In an effort to stabilize the economy, the government enacts the Cryonics Act. One hundred years in suspended animation, all debt forgiven, and a chance at a less crowded future are too good to pass up for John and his young daughter.

Except not everything always goes as planned as Sergeant John Crider finds himself pitted against a land of prehistoric monsters genetically resurrected from the fossil record, murderous inhabitants, and a future he never wanted.

Printed in Great Britain
by Amazon

19296208R00092